T ROOM

THE
T
ROOM

A Novel

Victoria Lilienthal

SHE WRITES PRESS

Published: 2022
Printed in the United States of America
Print ISBN: 978-1-64742-383-4
E-ISBN: 978-1-64742-384-1
Library of Congress Control Number: 2022901400

For information, address:
She Writes Press
1569 Solano Ave #546
Berkeley, CA 94707

She Writes Press is a division of SparkPoint Studio, LLC.

For my daughter

Tara Mantra

Om Tare Tuttare Ture Soha

A mantra is "a sound, syllable, word, or group of words that is considered capable of 'creating transformation.'"

— Georg Feuerstein, *The Deeper Dimension of Yoga*

WHITE 1 TARA

Across the street, a red bra on a mannequin in the Pink Pussy Cat's window features a naughty confluence of satin and lace and, like a siren, this bra in a San Francisco porn shop is calling my name.

Distracted, I cross Polk Street mid-block to take a closer look. I would like to imagine being less impulsive, yet here I am, standing transfixed on a soiled sidewalk littered with the cardboard remains of somebody's bed, obsessing about ways to please my married teacher/boss/lover.

Why? Well shopping is easier than attending to my own spiritual growth, let alone emotionally reconciling the empathic dissonance created by a rich and fertile tech industry and homeless tent encampments. Such are the daily visual oppositions of this city, my place of birth.

Undeterred by this, I step inside to find the red bra's twin on the rack and head for the dressing room. As my eyes adjust to the gloom, I shrug off my leather jacket and toss it on the floor. The black tank follows.

Strapping on the satin and lace, I assess. My thick brown hair grazes my derriere in skin-tight jeans. Pretty good. Not perfect. As if that matters when it comes to wielding my power; it does not. It's the stepping out from under my teacher's professional shadow that is freaking me out.

And, yes, I *do* get that this is actually a *changing* room. I *do* know better. I know the rules. Girl code 101: Thou shalt not fuck another woman's man. But right now, I can't seem to resist either the man himself or my own need to obsess over him, and—as if on autopilot—I therefore head to the register.

"Hope he's worth it," says the woman behind the counter in a voice that sounds like tires on gravel.

I smile carefully and cough up the bucks and change that I shouldn't be spending on anything, let alone another piece of lingerie, and walk out the door feeling that weird anxious high that comes from not listening to my better self.

As I pass Polk Gulch Books with its faded sign claiming, "HEREIN LIES THE METAPHYSICAL," my boot catches on that same sticky edge of broken sidewalk that the city never seems to fix—this feels like a sign. I push the door open. Inside, a guy sits on a stool in back of the cash register. Despite the clatter of a cowbell hanging from the doorknob, signaling my arrival, he does not bother to look up from his phone.

What a place. Shelves are stuffed with crystals and pendulums, everything covered in dust. I gag on the scent of sandalwood. It doesn't look like anyone has run a rag over this joint since before I was born, in my father's summer of love. And of course, there are books on subjects arcane and esoteric that, in spite of my interest in metaphysics, I have neither the time nor the inclination to read.

The Bay Area may still be ground zero for the New Age, but I'm really just a single mom trying to cultivate some professional leadership skills. My problem? My attachment to my massage therapist teacher. *Who in this relationship is leading whom?* I wonder a hundred times a day.

As I take a few more steps into the inner sanctum, something flickers in my peripheral vision. I turn to my left and look. Sitting on a shelf next to a bunch of tarot cards is a goddess with a little blue oval tag stuck to her base. Rimmed in silver, her tag reads *Made in India*.

I'm about to turn around and leave when another flash catches my eye, this time from the side of her nose. I lean in closer but can't find anything to account for the tiny spark; sunlight igniting a random piece of glitter?

Intrigued by the goddess, I pick her up and turn her around in my hands. Small but heavy, she is about eight inches tall, made of clay, and hand painted. Golden necklaces dangle between white breasts. Low-slung, neon-hued harem pants drape her crotch and lower extremities.

I turn back to Metro Man engrossed in his book beside the front door and ask, "Do you know the name of this goddess?"

He glances up briefly, moves his head to indicate his bored negativity.

I look back at the goddess resting in my hands. She has five small eyes—one each on her forehead, hands, and feet. She sits in full lotus, a position that—despite years of half-assed yoga—I still aspire to.

I put her back down on the shelf, pull my phone out of my back pocket, and intuitively Google the search words *Tibetan goddess*. An image loads with a picture not unlike the little figure sitting in front of me. Her name is White Tara. I read on to learn that she is the mother of all Buddhas, a tenth-stage bodhisattva, one of those *enlightened* beings. She represents the wisdom lineage of compassion.

Compassion.

OK, true confessions. It would seem I don't have much to spare these days. Recently, I made a disparaging comment about a female massage student named Star Child, accusing her of being "desperate." My daughter, India, called out my bad attitude. I apologized for my weakness of character, embarrassed that my kid had to give *me* advice on how to model healthy self-authority.

Then, as I shove my phone back into my jacket, a story pops into my head about a friend of my dad's, a man with no savings, who went to Wilkes Bashford, bought an umbrella for all he had left in his checking account—a material acquisition that represented the sum total of his liquidity. Why is it that I too have this irresistible urge twice in one day to abandon myself to shopping? Like right now? But most especially when it defies all healthy choice points.

White Tara blinks. I stare and stare, but she doesn't blink again. Excited by what I *think* I've seen, I instantly visualize her sitting in the massage studio across the Golden Gate in Marin—the one I rent from my lover/teacher/landlord in the Mill Valley neighborhood known as Tam Junction.

I turn her upside down and see that her ancient price tag reads fifteen bucks, a bargain! I obviously cannot afford *not* to buy this goddess!

My inner compass thus momentarily recalibrated, I head for the register and make my purchase. This time the clerk actually looks up and smiles.

"Want a bag?"

"Nope," I say, "save a tree," as I tuck the goddess away in my backpack cuddled up next to my sexy, new, red bra.

VERA

The next day, Sunday, I lay splayed across the flannel sheet on the massage table at my teacher's midcentury modern wood-and-glass compound up north in western Marin County, plotting my next move.

The acrid scent of Redwood Empire, "the only whiskey distilled in Graton, California," as my lover, Ernesto Archer, is fond of saying, competes with the scents of sage and melting wax from the white votive candles lining the windowsills. A view of redwood trees and grass fills the windows of the warm massage classroom, an independent structure complete with kitchen and dining rooms and communal Japanese soaking tub, built on a hillside with windows that open out onto a distant view of Tomales Bay. The whiskey in the cut crystal glass in Ernesto's hand catches the light as he sits there watching, waiting.

I inhale and roll up onto my knees. "I'm going to slip into something more comfortable."

Just shy of six feet, with curly brown hair flecked with silver, Ernesto sprawls on the massage chair as his black eyes appraise me, a look of raw appreciation spreading across his face. "Naked isn't comfortable, Vera?"

I don't answer. Instead, I swing my legs off the table and walk outside, barefoot, along a small stone path, twitching my ass purposefully. The gray Northern California afternoon nips at my skin, wet air waking my body up from its languor.

I enter a weathered yurt, lean over, and find what I am looking for. I strap on my new red bra first. A red union suit with its legs cut off comes next. Sliding the onesie over toned calves and thighs glistening with a massage lotion famous for its glide, I leave a strategic number of buttons undone for maximum cleavage. So too the back flap.

Rooting around in my makeup bag, I finger a tube of winged eyeliner but choose a charcoal-colored eye pencil instead. I stand up and heavily outline my pale green eyes, smudging my handiwork with my little finger without the aid of a mirror. Then, after shoving bare feet into my motorcycle boots, I stick my signature hat with its scorpion pin on my head and walk back to the massage room, ready to play.

As I walk through the door, Ernesto catches sight of my reflection in the floor-to-ceiling mirror along the entire back wall. Turning to face me, he rocks back in a pair of snug-fitting jeans. His features are alive. He's waiting to see what I'm up to.

I notice that he has taken down a picture of his wife, Jean, that usually hangs beside the door. The photograph is leaning against the wall on the floor, facing away. In it—as I know, having memorized the image—Jean's tall pale body is sheathed in black. Her face, framed by fair Pre-Raphaelite curls, can watch over us no longer. I can't help feeling the sensation the French call *la culpabilité*.

I cram my guilt, filed under Daddy Issues, Unresolved, focusing instead on my leggy reflection looking back at me. I want to give him plenty of time to appreciate me before I walk past him toward the massage table that stands at an angle in the middle of the room.

When I arrive at my destination, I bend over the still-warm flannel sheets with my fanny in the air, presenting him with a good view of my honestly lovely ass. We gaze into our mutual reflections in the mirror, before he walks over to the wall and selects a belt with a small holster off a hook. The belt holds a bottle of massage lotion, one of the tools of our profession. A massage therapist—bodyworker—by trade, Ernesto prefers to fuck with a bottle of massage lotion slung on his hips.

As he returns, I hear his soft grunt as he snaps it on and gives the bottle a solid pump. Hot hands move through the back flap of my onesie to encircle my waist, before he runs the lotion firmly down the crack of my ass, and up across my *raison d'être*.

He pauses and then gives my butt a swift stinging smack. Skin tingles as he unzips his fly. He enters me and sighs audibly using his feet to spread my legs even wider. I squeeze hard on each thrust. "C'mon baby, give it to me. Louder this time. Louder!" he orders, alternating between stroking me and slapping my ass until I yell, "Shaman! Yes!"

We look at each other in the wall-sized mirror, panting, laughing.

"I know I said 'louder,' but I think they heard that one in Kansas. This woman is changing the nature of the human condition, single-handedly, one orgasm at a time."

He is still rock-hard inside me. "The human condition needs all the help it can get," I say, sucking in air before rolling each hand into a fist, and extending both thumbs skyward making the thumbs-up sign.

"What the hell is that?"

"Double thumbs up mudra."

"You're too much. How did you know?"

"Know what?"

"Know that I have a thing for the Tool Calendar Girls I'd find in an auto body shop. The red union suit, the bra, the boots, the whole rig." He refocuses on fondling my ass again. "You've got such a great southern hemisphere, Vera. How do you always know?"

"Little bird?"

"Smart bird." He says as he slaps me again. I watch as he admires the white turning to red imprint that has most certainly been left by his hand.

"C'mon baby," he demands. "Again."

My hands grip the other side of the table for purchase.

"Tell me," he orders.

"Tell you what?"

He slams into me gently, fucking me in that way he knows how to do.

"Want me to stop?"

"No."

"Tell me."

"Why?"

"You ask me that question one more time, and I'm going to give it to you up the ass. You'd like that, wouldn't you?"

I would, but I don't say it.

My ass. My cunt. Oh god. I am so close, I'm mewing. I can barely speak English when out of nowhere my orgasm, like a powerful wave, washes over me and knocks me sideways. Impaled, I clutch the table, arch my back and claim it. "Hell, yeah!"

In tandem response, he comes. Our bodies go limp except for the dick. I can still feel it pulsating inside of me.

When he eventually pulls out of me, I stand up and turn to him immensely satisfied. I've never had a man meet me like this before, one who so gets me. In doing so, our sex has become secret and insatiable hunger.

"Here," he says, unbuttoning my union suit, "Let me free you, Tex."

"Tex? What is that?"

He pulls a shank of my hair out of my eyes and sticks it behind my ear. "Your new nickname. Tex. It's a good one, isn't it? It took me a while, but after this last performance I finally get your alter ego."

He peels the suit off my shoulders, down over my legs, and throws it aside before he unhooks the back of the red bra and releases my breasts. He picks me up and lays me down with my head closest to the mirror. My boots are still on as he says, "Now, except for the boots, you look just like a Modigliani."

"Aren't you going to take them off me?"

"No."

"Why not?"

"Because Tex likes to fuck with her boots on."

"You sound pretty sure about this aspect of Tex's persona." "Right," he says, "as it's exactly what I love about you."

I smile and roll onto my side to watch him undress with the compact agility of a ripped guy who enjoys being in his body. Save for his gorgeous black eyes, he's not a conventionally handsome man; no one would wow over seeing him walking down the street. He has something better, something more primal, less cerebral.

He drops his jeans, pulls a tight T-shirt off over his head, and tosses it on the floor.

He joins me and wraps his arms around me, rolling over onto his back and pulling me up onto his chest. As I move deeper into the cut musculature of his shoulders, I feel the flames that might be coming off them, like hallowed light, in the mirror's reflection, but right now I'm too lazy to mention it. As someone who channels—meaning I easily experience past life regression and altered states of reality, all this drug free—I have difficulty at times sorting out my intuitive gifts, and Ernesto is the first person who has ever tried to help me use my abilities in an organized way. I like to think he really does get me. Or at least wants to try.

He whispers, "I like my nickname too."

"The name Shaman suits you. Hell, screw the massage school. Why don't you just open a sexual healing institute? It's what you're doing most of the time anyway. I bet you'd have a lot of takers."

I feel him hold me even tighter. I know there is truth to my statement. I believe he is the real deal, that he is, in fact, a healer. A shaman: *having access to, or influence in, the world of good and evil spirits.* This is truly Ernesto, who works both sides of the human condition, the dark as well as the light. One of his specialties, among other things, is sexual healing.

"Why do you think the breasts and the genitals are taboo?" I ask him suddenly. "When I work across the pubis and breasts, women love it. I always ask first and will use the sheet if they want me to, but either way, they always say what a relief it is to have me honor their whole body—they get that it's all connected. People need to understand that there *is* a difference between sensuality and sexuality. Shouldn't we be more evolved as a species by now?"

I wait for him to respond, but he doesn't. Leaning up on one arm, I poke him.

"Somebody has to do it. A lot of people need this sort of help. Most people have never been taught how to be in their body, let alone enjoy it. We can do this, Ernesto. Run a clinic."

He pulls me back down on top of him. "You do know we're healing one another, right Vera?"

He's right. But I don't like admitting it. It makes me feel even more vulnerable than I already do.

Vulnerability is everything. Instead, I say, "You remember our past life in Mongolia. But you also say we go even further back than that. I don't remember the primordial part, but I definitely remember Mongolia. To collide with you again? Like this?" I spread my arms wide trying to take in the quantum enormity of our current human assignment. "What woman ever gets lucky enough to re-encounter her lover in another lifetime?" I pull him to me, kissing him deeply in gratitude. "I still can't believe you actually claimed me as your professional work partner during class," I add. "Thank you, Ernesto. This is a huge opportunity for me."

He did this. He'd suddenly called me his professional work partner while we were winding up the class last week. It happened toward the end of a demo with one of the students. I was standing right next to him, assisting when he singled me out. His wife, Jean, had come in late from teaching yoga and was sitting in on a vacant massage table off to the side when it happened. She managed to look detached as she received what was clearly a demotion. In the same instant, I was both proud, honored, and sorry for Jean.

She stood up and stretched, her lean legs looking fit. She's an older woman, maybe further into her forties than she looks, clearly not pleased about sharing the limelight with me. She shot me a look before she tossed her hair and swept out of the room.

If Jean was pissed off, it's understandable. She is, after all, the one who does all the grunt work for Ernesto, handling the books and bookings and details. It could actually even be her inheritance that built this place. She is the one who really deserves to be the magician's assistant. But here then is my secret: I don't want to be Ernesto's assistant—I want to be the magician.

Now as he runs his hand through his thick hair, he says, "I don't know. I must be insane, but I believe in you. You are a talented practitioner. Somehow, it felt like it was time to say it, out loud and in public, even if it was in front of Jean. Plus, I wanted to finally grab your hand and jump over that proverbial broomstick of yours."

I know what he means by my broomstick, jumping the broomstick being a rite of passage for marriage in some cultures. By claiming me professionally, he has created a formal bond with me in our work together, that ours is a marriage-like partnership.

But Jean has been his work partner and wife of many years. The same wife who'll arrive here shortly, so I don't have to take care of this man one hundred percent of the time.

There are some serious perks to having an affair, this being one of them. I don't have to get too close. I have my freedom. At least this is my convenient excuse when I'm lonely. I must have issues with human intimacy, or I wouldn't be fucking a married man, this being behavior, in fact, of which I do not actually approve.

"How do you think Jean is going to deal with it?"

"I don't really know. It won't be easy, but I'll make it up to her somehow," he answers as he cups a warm hand over my pussy, my flirty first chakra. "Call me an asshole, but right now, I'm more interested in this." He strokes me, enjoying my arousal, the nature of my instant response.

Once again, we each must work to push aside our guilt about his wife's feelings. At this moment, it feels good to be the center of his world. I really feel like I need his help to activate myself, but I'm not so sure how much I would like it if I had it seven days a week, 365 days a year. The only marriage I've ever had—the one that produced India—was a drive-by. I tried, but the guy just could not show up in any real way. I don't know what was worse, the lack of libido or the love affair with weed. I got out of our crappy studio in the Tendernob—this being the slum where the Tenderloin and Nob Hill converge—and moved back into my dad's house, on an alley off Polk. Two months later, in my childhood bedroom and hardly an adult myself, I gave birth to my daughter, India, with the help of a midwife. Not long after that, her father left town; we never heard from him again. Did this break my heart? Maybe. I was too involved in taking care of my infant daughter to really notice.

"Do you realize," I say, "that the word *collaborative* is the first word I wrote down on the list of qualities I was looking for in a lover?"

"When did you make the list?"

"A while back."

"What was the second quality?"

"Sexy forearms."

He extends and flexes his right forearm, musculature rippling beneath the dark soft hair.

"This pass the test?"

I grab his proffered forearm, bite down, and give it a juicy suck before looking up at the clock on the wall that reads 1:55 p.m. Reluctantly, I sit up.

"I'm late. Motherhood calls, and your wife is coming home to do your bidding."

"I won't let you go." He pins me with his arms.

I relax into his grasp. "You are a genuine polygamist trapped in a conventional marriage. I'm not the first, either, as we both know. Why didn't you two figure this part out a long time ago? It would have saved both of you so much pain."

"That I don't know."

"OK. Say I'm still here when Jean shows up, then what? We come clean about our affair? We all move in together? One big, happy poly-amorous family?"

I don't think he actually, truly yet gets that Ernesto-and-Jean remain the package deal that no one will pull asunder. It's not just about him being center stage. It's about them being married in the old-fashioned sense of the word, their being a real twosome, where—honestly—there is no room for me.

"I'm open to what happens. Maybe she could be too? I'm a lot," he says. "Even she knows that."

"You're fooling yourself if you think Jean might be into this. But OK, then, let's fantasize. You build me another yurt on the back forty. I'll furnish it with skins and pillows and ride in on my Mongolian pony sometimes, yelling, 'Honey, I'm home.' It won't matter when I'm here or not because I don't want to live in the big house. I'll want you to fuck me, but I need my freedom too. Like it?"

"You're making me hard."

I wrap my hand around his stiff cock. "Be nice to Jean. She works her ass off for you. I don't have time for all that. I told India I'd make dinner, so as usual, she's home waiting for me to magically reappear with a bag of take-out."

I let go of him and swing my legs back off the table. I grab my costume; then I walk back outside along the stone path to the old yurt where I've left my bag. Part office and part toolshed, it serves as Ernesto's man cave.

I find my jeans and black tuxedo shirt. The shirt has just enough ruffles to semi-conceal my erect nipples. Indolent, I go commando.

I have one arm in my leather jacket as Shaman walks in. He pulls me onto his lap into a chair by the wood burning stove and says, "I want you to listen to something before you go." He pulls his phone out of his pocket, types in the passcode and puts it on speakerphone.

I hear my own voice humming. There is silence, and then out of nowhere, I begin to belt out, "She'll Be Comin' 'Round the Mountain When She Comes." The sounds of my singing accompany what sounds like me washing dishes. I've butt dialed him by accident.

I laugh so hard I slide down between his legs onto the floor. He throws the phone aside, leans over me and says, "Say it, Tex."

"Say what?" I know full well what he wants to hear.

"Say it, honey." He leans over farther and wraps his arms around my waist.

"Ever play the piano?" Before I can answer, he says, "It goes like this," and begins tickling me.

"Stop!"

"Say it, baby. And loud." He tortures my ribcage.

"What? That I am yours?"

"Goes without saying. And?"

"And what?"

"And?" he digs in harder.

"OK! It's the best sex I've ever had. Is that what you want to hear?"

"Yes. That is exactly what I want to hear." He pulls me back up onto his lap and kisses me tenderly. Then pushes me back up to a standing position. I am about to pull the rest of my jacket on when he stops me. He puts his hands on either side of my face and kisses me again before stopping to take a long look at me with warm hands still in place. Finally, he lets them go and says, "Here, let me help you with that." He slips on the sleeve and picks up my bag as I walk out ahead of him wearing my old slouchy brown felt hat. A small Navajo silver pin in the shape of a scorpion is pinned to the hatband, a fat chunk of turquoise on its tail.

I am tall, my posture's perfect, and I love the sound of my own long purposeful stride. My boots crunch the gravel as I call, "Francisco!" Two dogs hurtle across the meadow toward us. Picking up the little one, I place my mongrel Frank's short legs on his Mexican blanket on the passenger seat of my ancient hybrid and get in.

My shaman grabs the collar of his big yellow dog named Luna. He restrains her from jumping on the car door as he throws my gear in the back.

He says, "Jean's dog. Isn't she a hypoallergenic stunner?"

I know what he's doing. He is trying to keep my exit *lite*. Something has shifted. We've both entered the liminal space of departure.

Still, I play the game and banter back. "Not my flavor, bestiality being exactly where *I* draw the line."

Ernesto leans into the window and kisses me hard, his dark whiskers welcome sandpaper against my lips. "Me too. See you in the Astral," he says, serious. He slaps my car as if this Toyota is the rump of my Mongolian pony because *it is* true—we actually do meet up sometimes in our dreams.

"But what shall we wear?" I ask, not waiting for an answer. I depress the silver switch and roll up my window as I watch him look at me through the glass. Sexual fantasy is a powerful tool. I love the foreplay, the after-play, and the in-between play, but here's the thing:

I love my freedom too.

JEN

I almost make a clean getaway when who should swing into the driveway but Jean, who rolls toward me behind the wheel. Embedded
underneath the impending chrome grill of her Subaru is a vanity
plate emblazoned with the word: MAVRICK.

According to Shaman's earlier calculations, she is at least two
hours ahead of schedule. I snatch a glance in the rearview mirror,
relieved to find him still standing in the driveway behind me. As he
begins to walk our way, I depress the brake in order to buy myself
some time before her arrival.

She pulls up alongside and stops. Once again, I find myself intimidated by this woman's luminosity. Earrings dangle like chandeliers
from her shapely white earlobes. Pale freckles, like a light celestial
dusting of stars, fan out across her nose and cheekbones.

She opens her window forcing me to do the same. "Hello, Vera,"
she purrs. "What are *you* still doing here?"

I hear Ernesto's voice through the open window. "We were just
going over a few things."

Jean's gray eyes continue to speculate. "Really?" She arches one
perfect imperial eyebrow.

Before I can respond, Ernesto leans his head in her car window

and kisses her hello. I watch as she takes one delicate hand off the
wheel and brings it to the back of his head. Long fingers caress his
curls with oval nails polished silver, shimmering like five moons in
the weak light. She murmurs something I can't hear as she kisses him
more deeply, and I'm thinking, *Thank god he didn't just go down on
me.* As I take my foot off the break, Jean cuts the kiss short, releases
him. "Drive safely, Vera," she says, as she glares at me.

"Thank you," I reply. I hit the gas and get the hell out of there.

It doesn't take a UN interpreter to translate the woman speak.
Bitch. My man. Not yours. I want to excuse my behavior with, *I'm
just borrowing him so he can help me reconcile a few daddy issues—
nothing about this says permanent condition.* But this, of course, like
so many of our thoughts, is best left unarticulated. Once out of the
gate, I swing south and settle into the unraveling stitching of the
leather seat. As I turn up Kendrick Lamar's "LOVE," singing along
to Lamar's poetry, "damn love or lust, damn all of us," my still warm
and rosy posterior is now in intimate connectivity with every imper-
fection on this road.

I look over at my dog and tell him, "Frank, the path to enlighten-
ment is full of potholes, and our shocks are shot, and we need a new
set of tires."

His limpid brown eyes look up at me while he keeps his head
planted on the seat, thinking, *Tell me something I don't already know.*

The road is circuitous and bumpy until Francisco and I come to a
halt in front of the green Highway One sign that reads "San Rafael,
San Francisco," the arrow pointing south.

Shortly before I met Ernesto, I had a dream about a man and a
woman from some ancient place—Mongolia?—where almost immediately this dream couple began making love. Their passion was so
hot that I half woke up and began touching myself. I was the one
doing the masturbating, but the inspiration to do so had not been
generated by me. After I came, I sat back, convinced that this orgasm

had just changed something in me, my planetary consciousness had been altered—anytime I've been on the receiving end of the multidimensional, I've ended up different. When the same thing happened the next night, I lay back a second time, feeling stunned. WTF!—this was the best sex I'd ever had, and I was having it alone. I sanctioned the use of my body as the instrument of the couple's cosmic communion, not that I felt that I had any choice in the matter. This love from another dimension—call it *astral* if you like—contained a force far greater than whatever dimension powers me.

A few days later, as I began to work with him, Ernesto described a chronic dream he was having about a man and woman in Mongolia. He told me, "It's uncanny but the whole thing feels so familiar. . . ." He looked at me questioningly. I didn't answer.

Later still, he confessed that the man and the woman were actually making love, that the power of this same dream was waking him up in the night too. Our nocturnal synchronicity was so profound that later I told him we were dreaming the same dream, aware that our truth as well as our desire would compromise me.

Now I've also done everything I told myself I wasn't ever going to do. Firstly, having an affair with a married man. Worse, waiting around for him to resurface from his marriage for the five or six days a month he works with clients in our studio called the T Room in Tam Junction.

Or even worse, leaning on him to help ignite my career. And far worse, causing his wife's feelings of jealously and insecurity. Particularly because she is on the cusp of being no longer young, I know this can't be easy for her. I assuage this last concern by reminding myself this man has a history of being unfaithful, that I'm just one more notch on the bedpost. Even so, none of this stuff can be good for me, karmically speaking.

After slightly more than an hour, I cross the Golden Gate Bridge and enter the north side of San Francisco. I gun it up Lombard, turn right onto Polk, and take a quick left into Pompeii. Our street is a tiny dead end at the base of Russian Hill.

At the corner, I catch sight of a man with a dirty blanket slung over his shoulders, lost and derelict, peeing on the base of a tree recently planted by the Urban Forest, the nonprofit India volunteers for.

Five houses in on the right-hand side, number sixteen sits back a little from the sidewalk. Francisco and I park in front of our little Victorian painted the color of dirt with some sooty white trim. I grew up in this house. Back in the day, one of my dad's sometime conquests left the infant me in a basket on this very same doorstep and—such as in a fairy tale—poof! Disappeared, never heard from again. Nor have I ever tried to find her. Despite the fact he was fifty-one when I was born and people mistook him for my grandfather, my dad raised me here right off Polk and left this now dilapidated house to me when he died. It's the only real home India and I have ever known.

Francisco and I run up the stairs and stop in front of the chipped front door to slide the key into the lock. I put my shoulder into it, but it's stuck. Frank waits while I kick open our door and then trots in ahead of me. Getting this door planed, along with a million other things, is on my deferred maintenance list.

"Hey you," I call. I take my boots off and walk barefoot into our large kitchen. Illuminated by the glow of her computer screen, my daughter sits in front of a huge plank of redwood resting on two trestles covered with books, sketch pads, and old coffee cans from my dad full of pens and pencils. Thick and burled, the cross-section of an old-growth redwood tree, the table he had made is surrounded by a bunch of mismatched chairs.

Unusually wide for a Victorian, my father made this room even bigger by knocking down walls in order to turn the first floor into an art studio. A potter by trade, he stuck a wedging table in front of the stove in lieu of a kitchen island. Later he set up a kick wheel with a small electric kiln in one corner of the room and stuck an electric wheel in another. He trimmed all his pieces out on our back deck, but I still grew up eating clay dust.

That's my childhood. I'm a free-range product of one of my dad's one-night stands, born on summer solstice, June 21st, the longest day of the year. Motherless, I was raised by him alone—regardless of his endless string of girlfriends—an atheistic, great, but alcoholic artist with limited family bucks who managed to make some cash as a potter in a more artistic freewheeling San Francisco of bygone days.

By the time I was a preteen, I'd learned to take care of myself, if imperfectly: self-care is something I haven't always been good at. I don't always make the best decisions or do things in a good, orderly direction, no matter how hard I might try. Like marriage. Like love. Like my professional life. Let's just say I didn't have great examples. But I did get one thing right: India, my beloved fourteen-year-old daughter.

INIA

I walk over to kiss India on the top of her honey-colored head. At five feet ten inches, she is already an inch taller than I am. She has her absent father's wide-set amber eyes, his tawny skin, her legs beginning somewhere just south of her neck.

"Hey, have you heard anything about this new virus COVID-19—in China's Wuhan Province?" she asks, not looking up from her laptop's eerie glow.

"Nope. Haven't been listening to the radio much; the world's just too unsettling."

"You need to, Mom. This virus could turn into a pandemic."

"Fabulous. To quote your grandfather, the whole goddamn planet is going to hell in a handbag."

"Seriously Mom, this is worth paying attention to. Like multiple ice shelves crashing into the ocean."

"Meaning?"

"Meaning it will change things. If the virus gets traction, a lot of people could die."

"Your grandfather always said there were too many goddamn slobs on the planet anyway."

"It's that kind of thinking that got us here."

"I'm too tired to talk about this right now. Too hungry too."

I go to our beater fridge and take out four ice cube-sized chunks of raw dog food composed of carefully calibrated ingredients. When I put them in his bowl on the kitchen floor, Francisco quickly devours them and smacks his lips.

I look at the open box of pizza sitting next to her and say, "Francisco is eating better than we are."

"I was starving, couldn't wait," she says, "Sorry!"

"I'm just kidding, honey." Unapologetically GMO, pizza sustains our life on a regular basis.

I grab a bottle of beer from the fridge and wander over to a daybed that sits under the west-facing windows. Exhausted, I collapse into a waiting pile of faded pillows and take a swig.

I catch India looking up at me.

"Mom, I need to tell you something."

"What, babe?"

Her tone is ominous. I may have just been off fucking my married lover on a Sunday, but basically I'm a good and vigilant mother. Possible scenarios assault me. Lost her virginity, it went badly, she picked up an STD. Tried blow. Some man tried to molest her. Or worse, she molested. India is only fourteen years old. Why did I let her spend most of this last weekend without a babysitter?

I'm about to prostrate myself on the kitchen floor in front of a tribunal of conscious parenting when India says, "Mom, I know you and Ernesto are hooking up. More than hooking up actually."

Astonished, I lift the bottle to my lips. Cold fizz slides down my throat and hits the void in my stomach. I can feel the effects of the alcohol instantly.

This is one of those make-or-break mother–daughter moments. If I lie about this, I set a precedent for lying. But being honest also means I am a total asshole. I bite the asshole bullet and answer, "Yes."

"Yes what?"

"Yes, I am, as you call it, hooking up with the man," I say and chug my beer in the ensuing silence. I look down, wishing I didn't feel guilty.

"But he's married, Vera."

I hate to admit that I love it when my kid uses my name. It's liberating as it seems to free me from convention, form, or obligation to act a certain way. I may like to think of my behavior as similar to that of a sixteenth-century Venetian courtesan, albeit with a twenty-first-century flavor, but even so, I'm not stupid. Not everyone shares this perspective. There are a lot of women out there who would not support my fucking another woman's husband, though many, many women have done it.

"I know he is. And he is not getting unmarried, otherwise known as divorced. I am OK with that. Nothing in your life is going to change."

"You mean you guys aren't going to move in together and live happily ever, blah blah blah?"

"No, sweetie. That is why they call it an affair. And I am not a bad mom, honey. I'm just an unconventional one."

She actually laughs—I can see that she is relieved. So am I. The drift of our conversation is more about how my affair with a married man will affect her status quo than it is about the rules. At least, I hope so.

"What's their deal, Mom? Are they polyamorous or something?"

I climb off the daybed and go to grab another bottle for fortitude. "No. That isn't what they're doing. He and the wife have a quasi-conventional marriage with its maybe conventional fair share of lies and lack of transparency. But I'm not the first one either. He's had lovers over the years."

I watch her roll her eyes heavenward. "Great," she says. "That sounds totally selfish and weird."

"I'm with you. He also claimed me as his professional work partner during this last class."

"How did that go over with his wife?"

"Not well. She looked pissed. I can't blame her. She works her butt off for him. I actually found her standing in front of the massage-room mirror muttering something to herself. She tried to look casual. But mostly she just looked furious. She quickly stuck something back in her bag."

"What kind of bag?"

"I don't really know, but Jean's fixated on it. She totes the thing around with her everywhere. I have no idea what she's got squirreled away in there, but apparently it houses the tools of her shamanic trade. She just completed a year-long intensive training in the magic arts—I guess this makes her a real shamanista."

"Perhaps it's really Jean," I think aloud.

"Jean what?"

"The one who *has access to or influence in, the world of good and evil spirits*?"

India tilts her head to one side. "Doesn't this freak you out?"

"Freak me out how?"

"What if she gets really desperate and uses some of that bad shit on you?"

"Oh, come on. You can't be serious. It's just a bag full of crystals and shit. If it makes her feel better, then what the hell. It's one more example of her giving away her power—"

"Stop judging," India interrupts me. She pulls a pencil out of the coffee can in front of her and starts drawing flowers on a piece of paper.

"Do I sound judgmental?"

"Yes. Do you think you might be competing with her for him?"

I walk over and shove a slice of pizza into my mouth as I think about Jean's behavior in the driveway earlier. "Hmm?" I say, mouth full.

"You didn't answer my question, Mom."

I pick up another slice and rip off the pointy end with my teeth, trying to obfuscate the question with a full mouth.

She gets her computer and stands up. "Listen, I'm going to go finish my homework." Her tall, thin form begins to recede down the hallway when she looks over her shoulder and asks, "Do you feel like we're finished with this conversation?"

We both burst out laughing. I look at her, feeling proud. My kid is so nimble, so poised, so adult.

"Ya got me," I say as I get up and walk over to give her a goodnight kiss before she runs down the hall with Francisco hollering, "Love you!" and closes her door.

To be honest, I'm a cheap date. Drunk on two beers, I jam a third slice of pizza in my mouth, aware of the nice big ball of anxiety that is now wedged in my solar plexus. As I try to swallow, I have to admit that India, as usual, is probably right.

VERA

The following Monday morning, I pull over at the drop-off in front of Fairview Prep on the corner of California and Presidio. India in the passenger seat, Francisco in back.

"What do you think?" My smarty-pants freshman of a daughter has a full scholarship and an internship interview at this excellent school I could never afford otherwise. She is wearing jeans, a vintage blouse, and a short, black, fitted jacket. A tiny gold-and-crystal micro-stud flashes in her elegant nose.

"You look great. Hip but official. Knock their socks off." I add, "Love you," as I hand her a burrito wrapped in foil, homemade and still warm.

"You too, Mom. Love you." She slams the car door.

Francisco reclaims his spot in the passenger seat, and we watch her walk into school. I linger because moments such as this make me ache with maternal pleasure.

There are worse commutes than driving across the Golden Gate Bridge to Mill Valley for work. With the Bay on my right and the Pacific on my left, I take in the view as in the distance fog cascades down hills covered in eucalyptus trees.

I exit at the Mill Valley, Stinson Beach off-ramp into Tam

Junction, grateful that the backup of commuter traffic is all heading in the other direction. I turn into a strip of shops to drop Frank off at doggie daycare. But when I open his car door, he gives me his saddest *why? why? why?* look, his liquid brown eyes boring into mine with a beseeching, *Don't leave me here with all this pain,* my dad's favorite line from Bram Stroker's *Dracula*, especially apt when Pop was hungover and feeling sorry for himself. Like when I'd had enough of his booze-fueled shenanigans and would slam the door on my way out and stay away for days at a time. I pick Francisco up and head out saying, "C'mon, Frank. Given how much dog care costs, I wish you could at least act a little more excited about being here."

I get back in the car, swing onto Shoreline, and turn right onto Tennessee Valley Road. Several turns later, I park next to an old house that partly obscures my part-time studio. The old metal mailbox is emblazoned with the number five.

First, I go around to the passenger side to collect my towel-wrapped Tibetan goddess, still nestled in back of India's seat on the floor of the car. Carrying my new acquisition in both hands, I enter through a gate at the side of the house. As I turn the corner of the walkway, I catch sight of the little cottage through the redwoods that I rent from and share with Ernesto. We call this cottage the T Room, "T" for Transformation.

The pathway runs across a small damp lawn. My boots brush through wet agapanthus as I bend under a branch of Santa Rosa plum propped up on a piece of bamboo. The fog is thick with the aroma of star jasmine. I pause for a moment to inhale the fairytale beauty. I take the last two steps up onto the sagging front porch and open the door.

I love this place. Covered in soft flannel, the massage table sits in the middle of the room like an altar with the head of the table facing the rear of the room. With white walls and old wainscoting, there is a fireplace with a stone hearth to the left of the table and a small kitchen counter with cabinets below it on the other. I set the goddess down on the kitchen counter and carefully unwrap her.

I build a fire and crank up the heating pad on the table. In addition to keeping the client warm, reputedly the mat is good for grounding and stabilizing the immune system.

I walk past a mirror hanging on the far wall in back of the massage table. The mirror hangs between a bed tucked into the rear corner of the cottage and a doorway.

I continue on through the doorway into the laundry room at the very back of the cottage, intent on changing into my work clothes. Doors on my right enclose the small closet that contains stacks of cream-colored sheets for the massage table as well as Ernesto's and my clothes. Jean is absent. Save for a couple of random photos, nothing of hers hangs in our closet. I guess you could say in a funny way when it comes to our work, we do live together, at least spiritually.

Black leggings and a gray yoga tank from the closet come out first. Next, I strap bands around my ankles—they're roughly three inches wide, Gore-Tex with Velcro closures on the outside of each ankle. These bands run the same juice as the heating pad on the table and help my circulation while I work, as their manufacturer claims, but mostly I feel like they ground me.

After pouring a couple of drops of a home-blend of eucalyptus, marjoram, and lavender oil from a small blue bottle, I rub my hands together hard, creating friction to warm them. As well as being my homemade deodorant, the concoction is supposed to be a throat opener. If my clients feel compelled to spill their emotional guts as a result of my armpits, well, all right.

When I walk back into the main room, the colorful statue of the Tibetan goddess sitting on the kitchen counter catches my eye. As I walk over to pick her up, I stop to look around the studio, wondering where I might like to put her. I'm not sure why I brought her here except I felt directed to. *Plus,* I remind myself, *I can always use more help cultivating compassion.* I perch her high up on the stone-and-wood mantel above the fire that is now crackling in the fireplace.

As I think back to finding her in that funky bookstore on lower Polk Street, in Polk Gulch, I Google a story about how Tara sprang from a tear on Avalokiteshvara's cheek. A Tibetan god, he spent the better part of his time clearing out the hell realms on earth, only to find that mankind refilled them faster than anyone could say *Namaste.* Now, as I put down my cell to light the votive next to her, I dare her to blink again, but she continues to regard me with that enigmatic smile.

I stare back. But as I do so, I flash back to a conversation I had with Ernesto the week before.

We were standing in the studio by the kitchen counter when he said, "I was going to bring Star into this next session, but then I decided that it was just too many people in the room."

I'd already heard about Star from Ernesto—an old student of his—but he'd never referred to her as a potential apprentice practitioner before. Meaning what? That she would come in and observe our work? This new piece of information bothered me. I tried not to sound petulant as I asked, "Why?"

"Because she asked me if she could get back in the game. The work. But three bodyworkers in the mix seems like too much to ask of any client."

Back in the game? I think.

"Well, I agree," I said aloud. Ernesto swatted my backside as he headed for the laptop on his desk, leaving me to consider this new ingredient on our mutual horizon line.

Now as I hear his footsteps echo on the walkway and he comes in the door I wonder, what exactly *is* his status with Star. He looks good in jeans, lace-up boots, and a leather motorcycle jacket lined with shearling. He dumps his helmet and backpack onto the floor.

He takes off his jacket. Biceps pop as he ruffles both hands through his curls. His black eyes twinkle. "Our eight forty-five just canceled, baby. What should we do?"

"What we always do," I say as I peel off my tank and pants. I zip off the Velcro on my ankle bands. As I slide onto the warm flannel, I'm already desperate for his touch.

He pulls a massage chair on wheels over to the head of the table and sits down to place hot hands around the back of my neck. Heat generating from his hands sears my flesh as he pulls lightly but firmly to lengthen my neck. "Oh, my god," I say, "Those hands. You probably run more juice than the mat I'm lying on."

"Think so? Hmmm." He falls quiet again as he works. Then he says, "Glad you like it, baby," before raking both hands luxuriously through my hair. Starting with my brow and working backwards, he massages my scalp, deeply. After a while he asks, "How was your evening last night with India?"

"She called me out on my affair with you." My teeth chatter a little. I still feel tender about last night's conversation but don't want to think about the anxiety that it provokes.

"Does she have a problem with us?"

Of course she does, I think, *my child is a moral creature.* But I answer, "She isn't judgmental. She has some questions about the ethics involved, given that you are cheating on Jean. But mostly, she just wants my relationship with her to be clean. It feels a lot better to me too. I don't like lying. But most especially, I don't like lying to my daughter."

"I get that."

Does he really? I'm not quite as in control of the situation as I felt I was yesterday while I was parading around in my new union suit. India knows about Ernesto and me. I may like being unconventional, but still I worry that her knowing about her mother's foibles can't be a good or healthy thing.

I take a deep inhale. I can smell him, part animal, part pine. When he begins to rotate my head, I blow raspberries through my lips and shake out my arms and my wrists. Next, I shake out my legs.

"Does the word docile mean a thing to you? Most people would be craving the massage I am trying to give you right now."

"My body feels stuck." I blow another raspberry through my lips. "Is this a problem?"

"Only if I don't get to do it too." He whips the chair around the table so fast it skids when he arrives at my midsection. He pulls the sheet down, leans over and gives my belly a loud raspberry with his lips. Then he lays his soft curls on my gut. He looks at me sweetly before he turns his head in the other direction and pulls down the sheet to reveal my short, cropped thatch. "Yes," he says satisfied, as if he has just discovered the El Dorado. "I am fucking the only woman left in Northern California with actual bona fide pubic hair."

"Old school."

"Looks like you need a new coif. Would you like that?" he asks.

"Umm."

"Would you like me to shave it?"

"Like what?"

"A heart?"

"An emoji? Ha! A smiley face?"

"How about a flame?" he calls back as he walks into the bathroom. Returning with a small towel, a straight razor, and a pair of scissors, he fills a mug with warm water from the small kitchen sink. "Spread 'em," he says, his voice going lower in command.

I feel him run the razor along the outside of a part of my body that is beginning to feel like the San Andreas Fault as he brings the patch in tighter and tighter. He sits back to survey his handiwork, holding the razor in his right hand before he leans in to make a few more alterations.

Thank god I still have pubic hair. He's the only person who has ever shaved me, and it feels dangerous. I love it.

When he is finished, he runs his hand downward over the newly shorn surface. I raise my head up to peer at the small flame left directly above my clit. "Like it?" he asks, not looking up. I can feel his finger begin to stroke me gently.

"Umm," I say.

I close my eyes and sink into the sensation evoked by his deft hand as he dips his finger into me and pulls it out. I hear him lick it and open my eyes again to watch him looking down at me as he stokes the fullness of a lower lip with a finger still wet with my juice.

"Don't go anywhere. I have something for you." He gets up and goes to the desk by the door. He takes something out of the pocket of his jacket. He turns to walk back and places a combination of slender leather thong and metal in my waiting palm.

The combination appears to be a necklace. I take the leather thong and extend it with both of my hands creating a big horizontal O as if I am playing cat's cradle. Once the leather has been extended, I can see two thin brass flames, each about an inch and a half long, hanging from two brass toggles on either end. "Is this what I think it is?"

"I made it for you, babe. Let me show you how it works." He pulls me off the table and leads me to the big mirror that hangs on the back wall to the left of the door to the laundry room.

"Put your hands over your head."

I raise my arms overhead. He slides the circle of slender leather over my hands, head, and shoulders, intentionally grazing my nipples before he installs it around my waist. When he lets go, the body jewelry hangs low on my hips.

I watch him in the mirror as he bends to adjust a toggle that rests about three inches just below my navel. When he finds the right fit the little amulet of a flame nestles into what's left of my newly shorn pubic hair. Then he moves in back of me to work with the other toggle that rests on top of my tailbone. He adjusts this until the smaller of the two flames tucks into the gentle beginnings of the crack of my ass.

Blown away, I whisper, "How did you know?"

By way of an answer, he picks me up and throws me over his shoulder. He stands there for a few moments enjoying the reveal of my wet pussy to the glass. I can hear him sigh contentedly before he gives my butt a resounding smack.

As he throws me down onto the waiting bed, he answers, "Bird told me."

GRCE

By ten forty-five, we are showered, dressed and ready to work. I am wearing my new body jewelry under my leggings, incognito. Underneath the pants, the metal charm tickles what's left of my pubic hair, reminding me that this man has claimed me with that flame. As I walk over to light a second votive candle next to White Tara, she looks back at me from her perch up on the mantel in back of the stove, almost as if we are admiring one another's ensembles. It may be my imagination, but she looks like she approves of it all, as return client Grace Sloane Watson walks up onto the porch for her session. The muscle jumps in his forearm as he opens the door.

Grace has been a regular client of his for such a long time that she has become a friend. She's a good-looking woman who looks better in a pair of slim cut jeans and a tight cashmere sweater than most women half her age. A woman after my own heart, she's wearing cowboy boots.

She walks in and flops into the chair next to the door. A tiny diamond is suspended from a fine gold chain against her smooth tan chest.

"Hi, I'm Grace," she says, shoulder-length hair swinging. "Excuse me for not coming over to shake your hand, but I just need to sit down. Good morning, Ernest," leaving off the *O*. I already like her.

"What's up, Grace?" asks Ernesto. The depth of the friendship between these two is obvious. Good friends, definitely. Or maybe there is something more. Does it bother me? I'm not yet sure.

She has also been kind enough to allow me to witness their work together, which makes their transaction feel all the more special. Until now I haven't had the opportunity to meet any of his close friends. I feel flattered as he looks over at me and says, "Grace, I would like you to meet Vera West, my work partner. Thank you so much for allowing her to be in your session today."

"Really?" she says and raises an eyebrow. Her eyes dart to a photo of Jean. "That's interesting, Ernest. I really don't know how much you're going to learn. Ernest and I just shoot the shit. I like having a man's hands on my body every so often. It's really no more complicated than that. I'm not interested in transformation, but I relish a good massage."

"Thank you for including me," I say. I too am the first one to admit that a really good massage can help anyone with just about anything. Maybe if I'd met him sooner, I could have avoided a few bad behavior patterns. I'll never know, but I like to think so anyway. This makes me something of a disciple.

Then Grace asks, "Have you two been following the coronavirus? The Chinese government is considering initiating a lockdown, very disturbing."

"Grace, we are *all* regularly about to die from something or other," says Ernesto.

"True. This time it may be very different. I advise that you all educate yourselves. All right, I'm now switching gears. I have a story to tell, so pull up a chair."

I've never seen a client so completely run the show. She is absolutely not in awe of the man or his abilities. Like good children, we oblige. Shaman settles into the massage chair by the desk. I pull up a zafu and plop down on its unforgiving surface—I'm happy to report that I have never meditated for a moment in my entire life, nor am I about to start.

"As Ernest is well aware, I've been single for one hell of a long time. Too long. I haven't been overly interested in marriage although I wouldn't turn my nose up at it a second time if I met the right man. Lovers here and there, I have not missed out. I've had a lot of outstanding sex. But more recently, I've had a harder time meeting single men. At least single men who are of any interest to me. I'm done with married lovers. I'm tired of being a courtesan. I want a consort. You know, a real man by my side? And I'm beginning to be afraid that I might not find one. So, I did something I said I would never ever do, so. . . ."

We listen.

"I went on Tinder and Hinge."

I want to burst out laughing. I love her. I want to be just like Grace when I grow up.

She looks at me. "Have you gone on? You're young and fresh and pretty—you probably meet handsome suitors all the time. But it gets a little harder when you're a bit older. I never thought I would say this, but I am starting to feel invisible. It is not as easy to meet attractive men as it used to be. But I am also old-fashioned enough to want the man to take charge of asking *me* out. Is that really too much to ask of these digital times?"

"I've never tried Tinder, Bumble, or Hinge but almost everyone I know has. I hear it's efficient," says Ernesto.

"Do I have to remind you that you are *married,* Ernest? Anyway, so I get on the damn apps, do some vigorous swiping, connecting, and match with a band of men. Just that part alone was a nice boost for my ego. Who knew? There are more single men out there than I imagined. All shapes and sizes. Some of them are quite attractive, while others. . . . "

She shakes her head, shudders.

"Tinder is tawdry. Still, a woman must be flexible. Being skillful in the art of traditional courtship, I sit back and wait for these men to make the first move. I start getting messaged by more men than I know what to do with. Then I meet someone who captures my interest via the app. Not in person, mind you. This fellow is away on business." She does air quotes with long tan fingers.

"We then arrange to talk on the phone. Well, I don't know what got into me, but it had been a while since I'd gotten laid. One thing led to another and there I was having phone sex with this fellow in Geneva. If he really is in Geneva. But the more remarkable thing is he sent me a picture of his cock. You have to see this."

She pulls out her phone, scrolls and shows us the screen. On it is a picture of a truly enormous penis. I am dumbfounded. I look over at Ernesto, wanting to laugh.

Ernesto does. Then he points to the screen. "What is that package of *beurre sans sel* doing in the shot? What's he trying to do? Create a sense of scale?"

"Hell, yes. This boy is hung," says Grace with admiration. "Either that or he wants me to slather unsalted butter all over his tower of power."

Ernesto laughs again. "Grace, wow. That is more than a mouthful. Maybe it is a good thing all you had was phone sex. You could have been injured."

Her handsome face erupts in laughter so deep that it comes from the base of her belly. "I know. I thought so too. I've never been with a man this large. It might require some fancy maneuvers. Perhaps some kind of apparatus? Like a crane that lowers me down on top of him like those horses that Catherine the Great was famous for fucking. I've been having fun envisioning the possibilities. But guess what?"

"What?" asks Ernesto.

"I never heard from tall, dark, and feral again. He sent me his penis, and that was the end of that. Now I am left with this photo as a good-bye present."

"How did that feel?"

"Fine. How often does a woman my age get sent a photo of a huge cock? I didn't have to do a damn thing. This cock came free of charge. Would I have felt better about his penis if it had taken me out to dinner? Hell, no. I'm a consenting adult."

"So maybe the better question is, 'How was the orgasm?'" asks Ernesto.

"Fabulous. Best orgasm I've had in years," Grace answers, looking pleased with herself. "Now get me on that damn table of yours, will you?"

Ernesto walks over to the head of the massage table and pulls down the soft flannel. I head outside ahead of him, barefoot, noticing that my ankle bands don't seem to be doing much for my circulation, my feet icy against the painted wood as he joins me on the porch, closing the door behind him. I wrap my arms around my gray yoga tank wishing I had a sweater on.

Standing with our backs to windows obscured by blinds that open into the studio I say, "I've never met a woman like Grace. Did she really take the whole thing with that guy in stride without making it personal? I'm not entirely sure that I buy it."

"She's a remarkable person. She's mentored me in my practice and taught me a lot about what it means to be a truly embodied woman. She loves good sex and makes no excuses. I have tremendous respect for her."

OK, so maybe she is just that evolved. Perhaps this is what happens later in life.

But I have another question on my mind. "Does that mean you two are lovers?" I ask, afraid to hear the answer.

"Not now, but yeah, we were." He looks at me. "But we were never into each other the way you and I are, Vera. But yeah, we did—we do—appreciate one another."

I digest this new piece of information. I'm not sure if I like hearing him compare our relationship to his with her.

"Does that information trigger you?"

"A little. Nothing I can't handle. I'm working with the sensation." I yawn.

"Keep it moving. Stick out your tongue. Say *ah*."

I stick it out and say, "Ah," but before I can stop him, he sticks his finger in my mouth, depresses my tongue quickly and activates my gag reflex. I gag and start coughing. "Do you have a license for that finger? I was joking." I hock into the bamboo off the side of the deck. "Satisfied? I can't believe you just did that." I feel like a little girl at the doctor's office.

"Do you feel better?"

"Actually, yeah." The weird thing is I do feel better.

"Remember, you transmute. If you are going to get hung up on emotional and physical sensations, then you have to clear them. You can't work dirty. These tools are simple. Given half a chance, the body wants to bring itself back into neutral buoyancy."

I don't understand what the hell he is talking about half the time, but it is this kind of mentoring that drew me to him six months before. That was when he announced that I transmute; that is, I am someone who is capable of using her body as a lightning rod to clear extraneous emotional material, not only my own but other people's schmutz. This is one of the reasons why I feel reluctant about being a channel. I mean, who wants the responsibility?

He calls this talent a gift. I call it a mixed blessing. Take me, for example. I feel everybody's feelings. My experience of being in my body is a chronic visceral experience, as if I am some giant walking sponge. According to this man, the trick is to "keep the energy moving." So much easier said than done.

"Hey, have you put any more thought into putting together that group?" asks Ernesto.

"A little," I say. But I don't feel comfortable with my professional aspirations right now. It's easier to talk about Grace. "Her story blows me away. Some women might have felt used, but she turns the whole scenario around. She isn't a victim. If anything, she sounds like she feels empowered. She's amazing. Is she always in the driver's seat?"

"She is. She calls herself a consenting adult. She chose to play with him in that way, and that was their transaction. She must be smart enough to know that the guy will probably call her again. Guys are dogs."

"How come guys are always the ones who get to say that guys are dogs?" I ask as he keeps his back to the door and quietly knocks.

Grace's voice calls, "C'mon in."

Ernesto puts his hand on the doorknob and leans toward me almost as if he wants to kiss me. "Because it takes a dog to know another."

He follows me back through the door, one hand appraising the tight curvature of my butt. I can feel his eyes on me. Grace is now lying faceup on the table. The glow of the fire in the fireplace to the left of the table highlights her bronzed shoulders against the cream flannel.

I walk to the foot of the table and take hold of her feet, using the sheets to make sure her feet are hip width apart. "Is the table warm enough?" I ask.

"Yes." Her eyes are closed. Ernesto washes his hands at the kitchen sink and holsters the bottle of massage lotion to his hip. He shuts the belt with a crisp snap before wheeling the massage stool over to the upper half of the table.

He takes his usual opening position and sits to her left. He rests his hands over the sheet on her left bicep before he takes hold of the back of her neck with his right hand. I watch as he puts his left hand in back of her left shoulder blade and pauses. He waits several beats for Grace's body to settle into his hands. Then he grabs her left scapula and pulls.

It is a small massage move, but effective. Blood visibly flushes to the surface of her cheeks as his other hand kneads the points on the back of her neck. Quietly, he explains that he is kneading her stomach meridian line, as if it were bread.

Ernesto always says never be in a rush when it comes to the body. Learning to be OK with not doing much, otherwise known as doing nothing carefully, isn't as easy as I am trying to make it look. Restraint has never been my forte. I practice keeping the pressure from my hands stable and consistent on her feet as I wait for her strong body to relax into the table.

Eventually, her head lolls to the right as she yawns and stretches. "Oh, my god, I feel so much more spacious."

I watch as he uses his right hand to loosen her jaw before returning to her neck. She heaves a huge sigh, reaching a hand to her face. "What a relief. That feels so much better. I am loath to admit it, but I've been over-focusing on my Tinder crush. Nice work, Ernest." She opens one big blue eye and gives him a winky face.

He moves her hand away. "Get out of my workspace," he says as he leans his head in close to her own as if listening to her anatomy. Either that or he is about to kiss her.

"Why don't you kiss me and get it over with?" says Grace.

I wasn't so happy about him leaning in like that either. Who is this woman? A mind reader? Like a panther, she cat-stretches before relaxing into a horizontal version of tree pose bringing the inside of her right foot to cup the inside of her left knee. Her arms lie splayed over her head in sheer abandon.

Shaman pulls his face back as his left hand begins to pull at her abdominal fascia, gently manipulating the tissue with the sheet. As he does so, everything about her body becomes heavier, quieter, and more rag-doll-like in my hands. I fold back the sheet and begin to slowly massage her extended left instep.

"Oh, yes. Have at it. I've lived at least three lifetimes, and my feet are tired."

Her strong foot feels good in my hands. In fact, I can't be sure, but I question whether the sex energy in the room isn't being directed more at me than it is at him, or maybe it's because of him? And here we are back to that old threesome thing again. Not that Ernesto would be opposed, but I'm not so sure. Not only am I jealous, I feel a little out of my league.

Out of the blue, Grace reports, "I have never met a man who didn't have a threesome fantasy." She gives me a wise smile as I cock my head.

"Vera, I know this thing between Ernest and me is somewhat confusing."

I'm thinking, *WTF?*

"Imagine your body is a tuning fork. Thinking that you are going to get lassoed into a threesome here with Ernest that you might not be ready for is counterproductive. If you're feeling insecure, you don't have to internalize your feelings. Identify and own your feelings. If your feelings are making you uncomfortable, it is important to find a way to release them. You have the power to choose what you want to hold on to and what you want to let go of."

"I know it sounds weird, but would blowing raspberries be a way to release them?" I ask tentatively.

"Yes! Like raspberries. If blowing raspberries makes you feel better, then, by all means, blow. It can give you and your body a moment to discern the difference between your actual desires and your fear."

"What does that mean?" he asks.

I had to agree with his question.

"Meaning sex is a basic desire. But we all have it for a lot of different reasons. Enjoy having sex for the pleasure of sex. I never have sex out of fear."

Shaman pushes the broad palm of his right hand against her breastplate and pushes her down a little, holding it there like he is trying to exert some form of control over the force of nature called Grace. I watch him lift his hand to work his fingers along the outside of her left eye cavity. He stands up to use both hands, leaning over her, careful to avoid that tiny muscle called the zygoma that floats along her temple. He explains that this work is designed to expand her peripheral vision.

"Ernest, I don't need help with my peripheral vision. I've got more intuition in my little pinky than most people will ever have in ten lifetimes. She swats his hand away. "Cut it out," she says. "Just give me a fucking massage."

He laughs, pumps his massage lotion bottle, rubs his hands together, and sweeps them from her pecs, down across her rib cage to take hold of her lean waist. In doing so he pulls the sheet down to reveal two very good-looking breasts.

"Jesus, Ernest. Why must you always spice up my session with a tit shot? I'm sorry, Vera," says Grace as she tries to pull up the sheet.

Her breasts look real. I want to know this woman's secret.

Grace answers me as if telepathic. "The secret is to know how to have fun, Vera." She looks down at her breasts. "Not so bad for midlife."

I nod in agreement.

"I try to trust my intuition. My advice to you, young lady, is to remember this: it has to—has to—be fun."

WHITE  TARA

work three more sessions with Ernesto before I grab my stuff and depart down the walkway. When I get in the car, I find a text from India: *where r u mom.*

Late again, late being the current story of my life. I spring Francisco from his doggie day care purgatory. Shackled, he yanks at his harness, toenails scrabbling, all thirteen and a half pounds of dachshund straining for freedom from this hell. He claims his blanket in the front seat so he can ride shotgun. We pull up in front of Fairview Prep. India opens the passenger door and pushes Frank, who hops into the back seat. He relinquishes ownership only because he loves her more than anyone in the world. And even then, only after she orders him twice. That is, *before* she gives me the one hundred and third degree about what she calls my *issues with chronic tardiness.*

Making dinner, I reflect back over my workday. It takes both hands for me to count all the times I felt insecure in the course of just one day at work. At least I have this much awareness at six fifteen on Tuesday evening. But I also realize that a goddess named White Tara sits up on that stone mantle in the T Room, just waiting to alleviate my insecurities. After all, I am the one who put her there.

"If only it were that easy," I say out loud. I swear a voice enters my mind. *Start your own group.* I look up from chopping onions in disbelief. There is no way a clay icon is actually talking to me, especially one that is in a studio across the Golden Gate in Tam Junction.

Then it dawns on me, whether she's giving me a long distance kick in the butt or not, I *can* start my own group. Immediately, I decide to create a group that will teach people how to transmute their feelings of insecurity. The only person who is holding me back is not, in fact, Ernesto, it's *moi* from Moiville.

After we eat hamburgers, India and I hang out at the table. India does her homework while I debate whether to invite some colleagues as a dry run for the group. As I sit back in my chair, I warm to this idea. I'm not sure what is going on astrologically. Not that I know jack about astrology anyway, but somehow it feels like it is time to say, *this,* ladies and gentlemen, is who I am. Or at least it's time to start thinking about it.

Boldly, I pick up my phone and call Ernesto. He answers, "Hey, baby," after the first ring.

"Do you have a minute?"

"Sure."

Harnessing my courage, I say, "I'm considering hosting a group in the T Room. Do you mind?"

"What a great idea. Feel free to run anything by me. Hey, do you mind including Star? It might be a nice way for her to reconnect with this community."

I do mind. A lot. But I don't know how to say so without sounding like a bitch. I settle for a lame, "I don't have her contact information."

"Don't worry about it. I'll send it to you just as soon as I finish unclogging the kitchen sink in the studio. I've had to call the plumber."

I volley, "Is this another version of yourself?"

"Ha! How do you always know?"

"Twin flames."

"You are so sweet," he says, and then he's gone.

I put my cell down and look up at India sitting across from me, face buried in an enormous textbook. "Don't most kids take chem sophomore year?"

"I'm good. My teacher says I've definitely been a scientist in my past life."

"Smart teacher."

"Mom, did you listen to what I sent you?"

"Hmmm?"

"*The Daily*, the podcast I sent you."

"About what?"

India rolls her eyes, "Jesus, Mom, *hel-lo*, the *coronavirus* that everyone's talking about?"

"I am not everyone. I am me, trying to make a living, trying to not be overwhelmed."

"I'm sorry, but you need to check it out. Listen to that podcast on your way to work." Then she asks, "How are things going at work anyway?"

"Pretty good. I've decided to try starting a group at the T Room."

"Cool. What kind of group?"

"I want to learn how to teach people how to own and release their insecurities via their bodies. I mean, everybody knows how to do it to one degree or another. We just don't realize that we know how to do it. I think it's one of the reasons why I end up feeling so emotionally backed up sometimes. I forget to transmute. If we all had more productive ways to offload our emotional stuff, maybe we could all be nicer to each other."

"I like it. You sure he's cool with this?"

"He said so."

"I'm a little suspect when it comes to him letting you branch out on your own. He's tossing you a carrot."

"Well, he did include one caveat. He wants me to invite Star Child."

"Wow. OMG, Mom."

"Yeah. Star Child is apparently her alias."

"I can't believe that these are the people that you *work* with."

"Honey, I wouldn't be working with her if he wasn't asking me to do so."

"*Right*," says India as she flounces out the door, skirt rippling against her thighs, tossing an *OK, Mu-thur* look over her shoulder as Francisco runs after her.

I holler down the hallway at what used to be our dog. "Traitor!" Both of them ignore me. She closes her door, leaving me to stew over my daughter's annoyingly accurate powers of perception.

Not long after, I go to bed naked, feeling like I could be coming down with the crud. It is later I become aware that I am dreaming.

In the dream I'm standing barefoot on the threshold of the door to the studio. I am wearing yoga pants and a tank. My hair hangs loose down my back. Ernesto's wife, Jean, is standing across from me on the deck, just off to my left wearing a jacket. With her right hand, she hands me a white paper bag with handles. As she does this, she says, "I won't be needing this anymore." I take the bag and open it. Inside, I find a large golden key. I take the key out and hold it in my right hand.

Abruptly, I wake up. My memory of the dream is so vivid that I almost expect to find a key in my right hand. I lie there feeling haunted by the dream. Despite being wrapped in a duvet and a couple of blankets, I am slathered in cold sweat, experiencing what I can only call an uncanny sense of dread.

The dream was brief, but I can't shake it. I realize what the bag reminds me of, Jean's bag. Both are the same size and shape. I shiver. This dream-time-real-time connection is just totally weird. But it's also way too early in the morning to focus on it. I burrow down into the soggy flannel, reminding myself to Google the symbol of that key before I fall back asleep.

The next morning, I never get around to Googling the key symbol. Soon I forget about it all together as I focus on my client work. It is now Wednesday, and I've managed to put a little group together for tomorrow, Thursday.

Star wants to show. So does another woman. This makes two men and three women including me. We're a go.

STAR

Thursday workday is uneventful, nothing until the evening arrives. I wind things up and look around the messy studio, feeling blitzed. Sure, I have a sense of anticipation about creating a new venue independently from Ernesto.

Everyone responding "yes" on such short notice says something, doesn't it? And I know I have something to say about transmuting emotional content. But as I strip the massage table and get out the mop, I cop to not really knowing what any of that is yet. In fact, I haven't organized anything. No handouts. Nothing. This is not my normal. My truth is, I do not feel prepared for my new group.

But these people are your friends, I tell myself as I put crackers and cheese and hummus out for snacks. As I line up the crackers in a circle around the edge of a plate, even though I am excited, I also feel a growing desire to skip the whole thing and go commune with my bed. I feel the beginning of a scratchy throat, don't I?

Like the tintinnabulation of a Tibetan temple bell, my cell dings. A text from Serena, my bodywork sister, saying she can't make it. This means that the only two women participating will be Star and yours fucking truly. There won't be another woman around to defray our potential for competitive energy, and there will be some competition for sure. I mean, she is already trying to get into this room as an apprentice of Ernesto's, if not for more. Suddenly I am not so sure about the wisdom of my choice to include her. I look down at the screen, feelings awhirl.

Mac arrives; then in comes Simon, would-be stand-in for Che Guevara, the '60s revolutionary style completed by a blue proletarian jacket and the bandana around his neck. He catches me up in a big, feet-off-the-floor hug, hoists me above his head, and spins me around a couple of times. He sets me down with a huge smile, proud of himself, the frisky fellow.

The singlet-clad, extremely buff Mac grabs me next in a bear hug, and they begin to set up an extra table. We are just getting started when, through the window above the kitchen sink, I spot Star marching down the walkway, determined look on her pretty face, her long, straight, dark hair dip-dyed on the ends in a startling shade of ginger. Along with leggings, she wears a hoodie that proclaims her allegiance to Philz Coffee. She storms through the door without knocking. She takes three steps inside and angles her body toward mine, simulating her version of the yoga pose Warrior One, left side forward. As she finds her center, she announces, "I did meet Ernesto long before you did, Vera."

"Jeez," I say. "Hello to you too."

I must admit that this is true. But the strident nature of her declaration interrupts the flow in the room and catches me off guard mid-sentence. "Love-fifteen" Star.

We all shift our focus in her direction. I look at Star's cleavage. My higher self knows this is a shitty thing to do, but my lower self takes charge with, *Hey, she didn't even knock when she let herself in.*

I watch as she sinks deeper into her stance and begins to recount all the "special times" she has spent here in *my* studio, in the company of my lover. Clearly on a mission, she releases the pose and sashays her bottom around the room as if she owns the joint.

Ours is now an extraordinary moment on the primitive battlefield of female competition. Dumbfounded, I make a feeble effort to counter her attack with silence, halfheartedly imagining that I am taking the high road. *I am his "work partner," after all*, I say to myself as she runs her finger along the T Room's kitchen counter checking for dust.

What a bitch, capital B. Not responding directly seems the *more* dignified approach. I decide not to meet her on what I judge to be *her level* and ignore her. I am about to say something regarding the structure of our evening (which I don't have the faintest idea about), when she interrupts me again, this time speaking over me.

I look at her and feel the balance of my personal power shift. I do not take the nature of her competition lightly. Instead of mentoring this young woman on how to let go of her insecurities around me, Ernesto, and whoever else she has stashed in her kitchen sink (I mean that is what this group is supposed to be about—hello!), I meet her need to compete with me with my own brand of poison.

I am angry.

I know I've learned somewhere that we're given a quarter of an hour to get our shit together: "In order to embody a true position of leadership, we must be able to course-correct our emotional bodies within fifteen minutes."

In order to pull off this maneuver, we must use something called "fair self-talk." For instance: "I forgive the idiot in me who created this group in the first place, most especially because I'm overtired and underprepared. Namaste."

But I'm no closer to an emotional course correction than I am to Pluto. Therefore, as the guys pair up to work together, I catch myself accepting Star's puzzling offer to work with me, mostly just to see what she's made of. Bad idea.

I need a massage, but this is clearly the wrong time, wrong place, and wrong practitioner. Inside, I know this. But why listen to my common sense when I am busy feeling resentful?

I thus lie down faceup on the table in my version of victim pose. And like I've already said, more than anything, I'm totally on fumes.

I glance at her as Star takes up her position at the base of the table at my feet. She pulls her hoodie off over her head to reveal a yoga tank that can barely contain the mass of her breasts. She throws the sweatshirt under the table before fidgeting around with the top sheet longer than she needs to. When her cold hands encircle my ankles, they feel like ice. It dawns on the troglodyte in me that, behind all the bluster and the competition, she is a very terrified girl trying to express her power tableside. Her shaking hands make it clear that she is struggling with her own feelings about female authority. Do I step in and mentor her by lending a helping hand?

No way. I need to let her flail.

Still, I sink into the table grateful in the moment to just be lying down when Star asks, "Did Ernesto ever tell you about the time we were in Sacramento?"

"Nope," I say. Then like the good competitive sucker that I am, I give her the upper hand and ask, "What about it?"

Star leans into my shins with her thumbs. "We were up in his hotel room doing a little bodywork when we set the heater on fire." She finishes the sentence and leans in farther to bring her hands up over my knees to grip my quads. As she does so, her breasts graze my insteps and rest on top of my turned-out ankles like a sack of rocks.

Eagerly, she looks at me, hoping for a response. When I refuse to ask why she was in his hotel room because the answer is so obvious, she climbs up on the table between my legs and bows her head. She sits on her knees waiting for my direction. Our current position would actually be funny—this is a moment for humor—or enticing, if I were at all attracted to this person, which I'm not.

I decide to personalize her behavior instead. I'm pissed off. I internally disparage the little girl in her who longs to be the center of attention and, therefore, special.

My gentle higher self knows this. But my lower self is so far from feeling gentle that, in fact, I'm just warming up on the subject when her cold hands sweep up my legs and encircle my hipbones. She holds them there for a few moments, giving me an intentional shot of the seemingly limitless chasm between her breasts. This is a crevasse a woman (or man) could get lost in, never to be seen or heard from again.

Star hops off the table like a baby elephant and shoves one hand under the sheet to cup my tailbone. She looks over at me as she starts rocking it. I feel seasick. But do I ask her to stop? No fucking way; I'm too busy feeling desperate.

I focus my thoughts on Ernesto and wonder what the hell he makes of Star's work as she announces, "I am going to give you a hip opener." She hacks away at my hip girdle with hands that feel like machetes. Her rock-hard fists crash into my I-T band like a wrecking ball. All this "move" manages to do, as far as I can tell, is torque a new and deeper level of my victimization. The woman is working me over.

My feelings reach their glorious apex when she pushes me onto my left side, hooks my right leg around her back, and uses her body to stretch mine—there is a look of triumph on her face, and I can't help but notice that sweat drips from her brow as I drop into the familiar minefield of my righteousness. I mean, what the hell? Righteousness is fuel. I know my way around this emotional map blindfolded. I can even imagine the outfit to go with it. And for sure it includes a pair of steel-toed boots.

This is what I use to get myself the hell off that table. My righteous disdain of this she-devil. Fuck learning how to transmute my insecurities. I use my own hands to stop Star mid-move, saying, "I am done."

I hoist myself off the table and lean over to grab my yoga pants. I don't even bother to look at her. How dare Ernesto compare my work with the dumpster fire that is this woman? I'm not even sure that he has made a verbal comparison, but he might as well have by urging me to create this dynamic. What an asshole.

In response to my defection, Star runs over to the pack she's left by the door. She pulls out a twelve-pack of White Claw and holds it aloft over her head like a trophy. "Who wants to shotgun a claw?"

Nobody says "yes," but she pops one anyway. She takes a long chug leaning against my kitchen counter, looking proud of herself.

When, mercifully, Mac and Simon begin to leave, she tries to calendar with the group for the next gathering, as if she herself had been the hostess. As she exits, she brushes by me with a breezy clutch of my left hand. I watch her ass pass through the door.

I wonder, *Where the fuck is she planning on having this gathering; she lives in Castro Valley. Or is it Gilroy? The garlic capital of the fucking world.*

I look around. The place is trashed. I feel like shit. I walk over to the kitchen counter and look at the White Claw, pop the cans, and— without ceremony, pour one after another down the drain.

Next, I reach out to Ernesto and call his cell. I leave a message saying that I've had an extremely hard night but that I am certain everyone else has had a good time. Then I ask if we can talk in the morning. I turn off the lights and go home.

The next Friday morning, as I am driving India to school, she asks, "How was your group, Mom?"

"OK," I mutter. My sore throat has settled in. I'm feeling boxy, hungover.

"You don't sound all that excited about it."

"I'm not. That parasite Star kind of hijacked the evening."

"What do you mean?"

"She rolled in the door, just so full of herself. I didn't have the energy or the smarts to put the group back on track after Star hijacked it."

"How could she have hijacked it if you were running it?"

I yawn. "My point precisely. I wasn't doing a very good job of running it because I was feeling pissed off."

"Why?"

"Because Star was freely *sharing* with us all her private interfacing with Ernesto."

"Wait, what does that mean? Is she having an affair with him too?"

"No, but she has had a moment or two with him in the past. I have no clue why he made me invite her."

"Because it's Ernesto, Mom," my daughter says. "And because she's Star, she needed to tell you about it, right?"

"Yes, while I was lying on the table receiving a crappy massage from her. No wonder I feel like I went ten rounds."

"What did she say?"

"She told me how they were both in Sacramento and how they were in a hotel room and maybe something got draped over a heater and it caught fire. According to her, it was because, 'it was all so *hot.*'"

"Ew. I might get sick," my daughter says.

"Direct quote."

India bursts out laughing. "That is hilarious."

"What do you mean?"

"I mean, first of all, the story is completely stupid. She was telling you to 'watch the fuck out, bitch.' I wonder why."

"Do you mind putting that in plainer English for those of us who are a little slow on the uptake this morning?"

"Oh come on, Mom. You know what she was doing. She was marking her territory. Girls do this all the time. It's not healthy."

"She was definitely throwing her weight around, and, given the size of her ass, she was doing a pretty good job. Also, her bodywork so sucks."

As we pull up in front of her school, India finishes with, "Vera. Body shaming? Seriously? You are a healer. You're bigger than Star whatever her real name is. You also have to ask yourself why Ernesto made you invite her. It was a setup."

"My hangover just got worse," I say as I hand her a tuna fish sandwich wrapped in brown wax paper. "I can't even believe I made this for you, given the delicate nature of my condition."

"Thank you. Love you! I hope you feel better."

And she is out of the car, loose honey-colored hair dangling above a thrift crop T-shirt of some hip band from the seventies, a pair of black jeans, Converse high-tops on her size sevens.

Frank jumps into the front seat, tail wagging. "Do you agree with her, too?" I ask him.

He looks back at me and smiles wisely. "See," I say as I pull away from the curb, "everyone in our household is more evolved than I am, Frank. Even you."

GRACE

Since I don't have a client until eleven thirty, I drive home to repair my psychic infrastructure. When I finally do connect with Ernesto by phone, he says, "I hear that the evening was a success."

Perplexed, I ask, "How do you know?"

"I just got off the phone with Star."

"Why did you consult with her first about an evening that I arranged in our studio?"

"I didn't. She called *me* to talk about it. I wanted to get a circumspect opinion."

"I liked you better in our last life!" I yell and hang up on him.

Of course, he calls me back right away, but I refuse to answer. I crawl back into bed with my sore throat and the rasps of my voice. I am now having considerable trouble resetting my leadership button.

I decide to call Star's metaphysical female embodiment "the harpy," proud of myself for her new name. Harpy eagles, they are symbolically defined as the evil female of cosmic energies. Perfect.

I've fixated on her lack of respect for me. It's so much easier and, yes, even malicious to focus on Star than on myself. According to India, I know that, as a healer, this deflection is not appropriate. But I'm at a particularly juicy moment in my personal devolution. I am suffering, as I build my case for my victimhood, stone for stone. Things are not progressing according to *my* divine plan.

The next time my phone chimes I answer, feeling grumpy. "What's up, honey? Did I miss something?" comes his voice on the other end.

"It really bugs me that you had me invite Star and then spoke with her first about my group."

"This wasn't done on purpose."

"What did you even mean about getting a circumspect opinion? I would hardly call hers circumspect. All she did was spend the evening telling me about how much fun she had fucking you with a flaming heater next to the bed."

"She told you that?" I can almost hear him chuckling.

"It's not funny. Why didn't you tell me you two were lovers?"

"We aren't lovers. We may have had a moment—that's all."

"Not according to her. Apparently, you've had quite an impact on her."

"Listen, I have an idea for you."

"What?"

"Running your own group isn't so easy. Believe me. I think you can use some mentoring from someone other than me. What about an older woman? How would you feel about being mentored by Grace?"

Flattered, I answer, "She's such a good friend of yours. I love the idea. I really like her. Do you think she might be interested?"

"I know she's interested. She likes you too. She said so when she called me the other day. Why don't I call her right now and call you back?"

"OK." I disconnect.

Moments later my phone chimes. I answer.

"You're on. She's going to call you in a few minutes. She sounds really happy about the idea. I know you two are going to get along. I've got to get going."

"Can I ask you a question first?"

"Hit me."

"Is there anybody you haven't fucked?"

"That depends on your point of view. What do you want me to say, honey? Nobody is better than you?"

"Yes."

"Well, that is true, Vera."

"Thank you. Given your level of connoisseurship, I take that as a compliment. I can't wait to talk to Grace, even though I feel a little intimidated by her."

"Don't be. You two are complementary. She's just older than you are and has more living under her belt. Gotta run, babe."

I feel my hangover dissolving. I get out of bed and pull myself together, having to admit that, despite the fact that Star is trying to park her posterior in my studio space, things are looking up.

Not long afterward, my cell chimes. Grace. I try sounding professional. "This is Vera West."

"Good morning, Vera West. Grace Sloan Watson here. I just got off the phone with Ernest. He says you can use a little guidance. I'm not sure if I'm the woman for the job, but I'm happy to offer my services."

My face flushes with girl-crushing on Grace. "I am beyond thrilled," I gush.

"Likewise. What are you doing this afternoon? Remarkably, I am free. Would you like to come over to my house for tea? Hell, fuck tea. Let's have a drink. Are you free?"

"Where do you live?"

"I'm in Pacific Heights. Where are you?"

"I'm at the base of Russian Hill on an alley off Polk Street. But I'll be coming from the studio. I can make it to your house by five thirty. Will that work?"

"Perfect. I'll text my address. See you later." She disconnects. Immediately my phone dings: 2920 WASHINGTON STREET

I text back a bland "ok!" not wanting her to know I'm so excited I can hardly stand it.

I text India:

WON'T BE HOME TILL ROUND 6:30ISH TONY'S TONIGHT?

I grab Francisco's lead and start whistling again as I head off to work. I hang in there working with clients until the last half-hour to go when I find myself feeling impatient. The minute the feet of my last client hit the wooden walkway, I strip down, jump into the shower, lather up, and rinse. I step out—skin pink—to pull on my civilian clothes. Armed with my motorcycle boots and leather jacket, I pick up Francisco and jam for the city.

I'm just early enough to find parking in front of what Grace calls her house, which is actually a mansion with an imposing stone-colored stucco façade sitting in back of a wall the same color with a wrought-iron gate. My new mentor is clearly not worrying after what my father called the wherewithal.

Looking down at Francisco on the dirty leash he pees on regularly, I straighten the straps on my camisole shirt first before using both hands to smooth out my hair. To my left is a doorbell and a keypad with an intercom.

After I buzz, I hear a voice with a French accent ask, "*Allo?*"

"Yes, this is Vera West."

"One moment please." As the gate buzzes, I push. *Click*: it opens, and Francisco and I step into another world.

White roses wind along the stucco walls as I climb steps to a portico sheltering the glossy black front door. A large brass circular knocker adorns the formidable surface. I lift my hand to knock and stop in midair as the door opens to reveal an attractive man, thirtyish, wearing a white button-down shirt with slim black tie, black pants, and black shoes. *You have got to be kidding me.*

"May I take your coat, mademoiselle?" he asks in such an impossibly French French accent it sounds like comedy.

I hand it to him, wondering if this guy is a for-real butler and who the hell has a butler anymore? Evidently he is one, as he charms me with, "Madame is waiting for you in the library."

I follow him across an entryway of highly polished black-and-white-diamond floor tiles. Francisco's toenails click on the surface as the butler leads me to an archway on the left and gestures for me to take the two shallow steps down into an enormous white room with a huge glass-and-metal skylight. Astonishingly retractable, it is partly open.

In the most beautiful room I have ever seen, Grace sits on a long pale-gray velvet sofa, with a golden retriever with a very white muzzle sleeping next to her. Above her is an enormous photograph of what looks like the interior of a dilapidated opera house in some historic European nation. It takes up the entire wall behind her and hangs between two windows looking west. The windows are impressively shrouded in what must be ten thousand yards of silver Thai silk.

The wall across from her holds a large fireplace flanked by two enormous dark metal floor-to-ceiling bookshelves. Both have sliding dark metal ladders like the kind I've seen in a fancy bar to get bottles of booze off the highest shelf.

Suede armchairs sit on either side of the fireplace. There are more on either side of the sofa. In the middle of the seating arrangement is a large low glass table on a dark metal base covered in coffee table books. One in particular is deep blue with a picture of a large golden Buddha on the cover. Something about it catches my eye. Looking north the wall is entirely glass, revealing her breathless view of the Bay, Alcatraz right there, Marin beyond.

Grace's voice breaks my spell. "Come sit down, Vera. I am so glad you brought your little man. What's his name? Shamus needs visitors even though he really can't see or smell anything anymore." She pats him lovingly. Her golden dog is sitting on fabric that likely costs as much as India's tuition.

I walk over feeling underdressed in my scuffed motorcycle boots and jeans to sit in the soft suede of the armchair located to Grace's right.

"I'm having a glass of mezcal. A friend of mine makes it in Oaxaca. Would you care for some?"

What will this woman come up with next? She drinks mezcal. She gets sent large cock pix by unknown men. She wears jeans and cowboy boots, a loose white silk blouse, and lives in a fucking chateau.

"Yes, please." I watch her steady hand as she pours me a glass.

"Here, have a cheese coin. Francois just made them today—delicious." She passes me a tray of round little crackers the color of cheddar.

I take one and pop it in my mouth. Crisp, I can taste cayenne. It is somehow the perfect addition to my first smoky sip of mezcal.

"He is not my lover if that's what you're wondering."

I haven't even gotten that far yet. I am just trying to catch up to being in this woman's fairy tale. Before I can even stop myself, I burst out laughing. "Too bad," I say. "Which one, Ernesto or Francois?"

Grace nods. "I knew I liked you, Vera. You didn't get to say too much last time I saw you. Not that you had a chance. Ernest always has to be the center of attention. But I can tell you have something. I like that in a woman. And, just FYI, never fuck the help."

All I want to say is, *Who are you?* I've never met a woman like this and hope I get to meet more of them.

"Guess what," she says mischievously as she lifts the small crystal glass to her lips.

"What?"

"I am certain you are dying to hear about the next installment of my adventures with the man and his glorious cock. Naturally, he did call. Men always do. Since he didn't get back to me in a timely fashion, I didn't respond. I admit I enjoyed the phone fuck. Does this make me a slut? I hope so. Being a slut is so good for the female morale. Still, a gentleman sends flowers."

With two long fingers she selects a cheese coin and nibbles it. "I think this is very modern of me, don't you agree?"

"In what way?"

"Sexting. Everybody is so damn busy these days. Who actually has the time to climb into bed together anymore? I'm rarely in the same time zone from day to day myself."

"Lots of people send pictures."

"Not I. I don't have that much faith in the cloud. Plus how do I take a really good-looking picture of my pussy without one of those stick things? This takes the selfie to another level that I'm not prepared to commit to. I've never even tried, though he keeps asking me to. But my philosophy is, if he wants it that much, he can damn well come and get it. Men always love a good chase. This is plain old procreation one-oh-one, no matter how old anyone is."

Diamond studs flash in Grace's ears as she pours herself more mezcal. I look at her feeling, like I've died and materialized to find myself in female mentoring heaven.

"Ernest said you feel like you can use some mentoring. I don't know if I know exactly what it is you're looking for, but I'm happy to be of service."

"I think just being with you is a form of mentoring. I'm in a little over my head with Ernesto."

"Why? Because the two of you are lovers?"

Mid-sip, I restrain myself from spitting my mezcal out all over her glass coffee table. "Did he tell you?"

"I've been around the block, my dear Vera. I could smell it the minute I walked in the door. The chemistry between the two of you is electric. Besides, he never works with anyone he isn't fucking. And I do know you know that. Ernest has fucked everybody, not just famous in this regard, but notorious. But it's also the first time

I've heard him call anyone his work partner before except Jean. This bothers me. It's unsettling."

I don't know how I feel about this new piece of information. Suddenly I feel bold. "So what about you?"

"Of course, darling. He is a tantalizing morsel. But just for nibbling on. He's a little too big for his britches for my taste. Plus, I like a man with more seasoning under his belt. And as we have already established with my friend from Geneva, I have a weakness for the unusual."

I feel like a crappy conversationalist, but I just can't return the ball quite as fast as she can hit it. Not yet anyway.

"Listen, Vera, I have a dinner this evening. I know Ernest sent you here to talk about a group you're developing, but I want you to really hear what I'm about to tell you about Ernest. He is a handful. I don't know what's going on between the two of you, but I don't want to see you get hurt. Don't put all your eggs in that basket with him. Keep your options open. Enjoy him, but don't depend on him—I hope you know what I mean."

"What makes you say that?"

"I've known him for a long time. He got married early in college. You've met Jean? She is older and basically runs the show, even though he makes a big deal about being in charge. She likes to give him just enough rope. I'm his friend, but regardless of his considerable charisma, he's a real shit disturber. He will never leave her, so don't expect him to."

"Actually, I don't want him to. I like things the way they are. I like being his work partner."

"Those first two comments make you a more interesting woman to me. But honey, what you need to really understand is that it's Jean who is his work partner."

"She doesn't do bodywork."

"It doesn't matter. She is his wife and life partner. You must understand this." Grace pauses for a moment before continuing. "Consider this: Perhaps your story with *Ernest* isn't just about him, or even your idea of your love. It's actually about you and Ernest and Jean."

"What do you mean?"

"Well, it certainly could be a more provocative reason for your participation in this love triangle than simply competing with her to be his work partner. . . ."

I can't help interrupting her. "I *am* his work partner! She doesn't even do this work."

Patiently, Grace holds up one long slim finger. "Please let me finish. Your job is to learn how to stop comparing your experience to hers. Do you want to know why?"

I nod reluctantly.

"Every time you compare your experience to hers, you are competing with her. When you do this, you are using something to measure, say it's a ruler, to quantify what love looks like and who gets more of it. Ernest makes you his work partner, then what? You are the winner? Is that how it works?"

I feel like Grace has me in a cosmic headlock. I barely nod yes.

"Good," Grace responds warming up to her subject. "They have their own transaction around this whole thing. It was in place before you ever showed up. Maybe this is something that he does with women in general? Maybe he likes to pit them against each other so he can be the center of attention? It's definitely something I've seen other men do too. Sometimes they like to play women off each other like a rooster in a henhouse. Our job is to be smarter than that."

I'm too distracted by everything Grace has just said to even imagine what Ernesto is wearing while he is in the henhouse. "My thing with Ernesto is different. I don't know what else to say. It just doesn't fall into a conventional relationship box."

"It may be different, and it may be special, but in a lot of ways what you're playing out with them is nothing new."

Suddenly, I am exhausted. Why am I so much more tired when I work these days than I used to be?

Grace must notice my fatigue when she says, "This is the last thing I am going to say: Imagine life is like a play. You and Ernest and Jean are all characters in this play. This makes Jean a foil for you. You get to play off of her and any other woman who comes into Ernest's field, for that matter. Star, for example."

"He told you about Star?" Confused I say, "I am not sure I follow."

"Yes, he told me about Star. Star—or more importantly, Jean—reflects all your feelings about what it means to be a woman. They are both here to help you heal your feelings about women in general."

I want to say, *You're shitting me, right? You and India are ganging up on me.* But I don't. Instead, I keep listening.

"I wouldn't put too much faith in what he says either. Watch out for those two. I've seen them do this threesome dance before. I think it turns them on. But not in a fun way. It's more vampire-like. Everything about Ernest is about Ernest first. No matter how good your pussy feels with him, always keep this in mind."

Grace stands up and makes a gesture for me to walk in front of her. Shamus jumps off the sofa and stretches. Crotchety, he comes over to sniff Francisco, his feathery tail wagging. He pads along next to Grace as she walks us toward the front door.

"I like you, Vera. Come back and see me whenever you please. And in the meantime, I want you to know that I am going to keep my eye out for you. I'm on the lookout, OK?"

Immediately upon hearing this, I feel myself relax. I've never had anyone, especially a woman, say something like this to me before. Her words touch me. As I go to thank her, she catches me up in a warm hug.

"Good-bye, Vera. Remember to take good care of yourself."

I begin to descend the stairs, and turn back up to see her standing in the doorway looking sleek and beautiful with her dog by her side.

I wave, feeling like I may be in good hands for the first time in a long while. Then I pick up Francisco and take the rest of the front stairs two at a time, inhaling the aroma of Grace's espaliered white roses.

VERA

'm feeling elated from my drink with Grace as Francisco and I pull up in front of our little house on Pompeii. From its position in the cup holder, my cell dings with a text. Ernesto: *surprise i'm at the studio you free?*

I stare at the screen. Why? Why? Why do I lust after this man? Why do I still want to ride him bareback all night long? I consider my ensemble. A suede halter and G-string should do it. Some feathers tied in my hair and maybe even a blackened front tooth simply to test his tolerance for the absurd. So much for the quality of Grace's mentoring.

But I cannot/will not blow off India. I text back: *sorry pizza night with India. maybe later*

My phone dings: *take your time baby*

When I get Francisco out of the car, he races ahead of me up the stairs to wait by the front door. We shove in and walk down the hall to the kitchen and find India sitting at the table with an empty glass and a quart of chocolate milk sitting next to her.

"I'm starving," she says. "Can I call Tony's?"

"Yep. Can you order a Caesar salad, too, please?"

After she calls, India asks, "How did your mentoring meeting go?"

"So good. Grace lives in a palace in Pacific Heights. She has a hot French butler who makes these crispy little cheese coin crackers. It's heaven. I think even you would like her."

"Did she give you any tips on working with Ernest?"

I can't resist the laugh that's bubbling up. "For one thing, Grace refuses to use the 'o' on Ernesto too."

"She sounds awesome!"

"Can we please just eat pizza tonight together and not discuss anything meaningful or heavy—like COVID-19—or healthily dietary?"

"Wake up to the planet, Mom. It's got its own agenda right now. And yes, Grace will be helpful too."

"Why do you keep saying that about Grace?"

"Because you are hanging out in an ongoing relationship with a married man. Really, Vera, if he were single, would you still be interested? I think there's something about that triangular dynamic that attracts you to it."

Just then, the doorbell rings. Francisco hurls himself out of his dog bed, barking. I fish my wallet out of my purse. "I am pleading with you, can we just eat pizza? And BTW, I might head out later tonight to see him."

Buddha-like, India smiles back at me as I dash for the front door. I restrain Francisco with my right foot as I tip the guy. When we return to the kitchen with the pizza, Frank trots along beside me looking pleased with himself.

We eat. Then we spend the rest of the evening doing what we do when we are not having meaningful discourse. We bake chocolate chip cookies while cruising around a bunch of clothing sites, online shopping for India's dress for Winter Formal.

Later, I tap my fingertips on India's door. "I'll be back in a while, sweetie."

"OK," comes the voice from inside her room.

My heels click softly on the hardwood floor of the hallway as I try to sneak out of our house, wearing a vintage trench coat with thigh-high, black suede boots. My hair is swept up into a messy chignon. I've even taken the time to apply winged eyeliner, mascara, and flame-red lips.

I almost get to the car undetected when India opens the front door and yells, "Aha, just as I thought!"

I stand next to the driver's side holding a plate of homemade chocolate chip cookies, looking guilty as charged.

"Hey, where ya goin' with the cookies?"

"I'm just going over to surprise him. I won't be too late."

"What do you have on under the trench coat?"

"Something uncomfortable." I look down and fumble around with my keys.

"Sure. Fine, but hey, Mom, it's nowhere near Halloween."

"I know. I just thought I'd get a jump on the holiday!" I'm trying to sound as playful as she is as I hop into the car. Secretly, I am embarrassed to have my daughter witness such need.

I pull a U-e and wave as I make a fast getaway. But not before I start asking myself what any grown woman worth her salt should be asking herself.

Why am I wearing this trench coat? And in front of my teenager? I pull over to look at my cell as if some sign from the universe will magically appear on the screen. I look down at my thighs. Am I really wearing black silk stay-ups, a very pretty, transparent black lace bra, and the skimpiest thong known to mankind in order to bring this married boss of mine a still-warm plate of chocolate chip cookies, a man's ultimate mistress fantasy? What's in all this for me? Like, why am I performing? After a moment, my common sense gets the best of me, and I decide to head home.

Once inside, I stop outside India's door. I tap.

"What's up? Did you forget something?" comes her voice from

inside her room. I can hear feet walking across squeaky floorboards.
She opens her door.

"Nope." I extend the platter toward her. "Care for a cookie?"

She selects one and bites into it, watching me. She licks the still
warm chocolate from her lips.

"You were right," I confess. "I just checked my calendar. I must
have been confused. Today is *not* Halloween."

WHITE 11 TARA

The following Monday, dead tired, usual drill. I drop India off at school and drag Francisco—whining—into daycare. He gives me one last guilt trip look as his young and cheerful female handler takes him away. I've done a full tour through this joint and happen to know all the people who work here. I'm absolutely certain, beyond any doubt, that my dog is not suffering. In fact, he's another male who is manipulating me.

Annoyed, I swing onto Tennessee Valley Road. Already dressed for work, I stride up the pathway to see a tall, dark-haired man. He stands outside, on the porch, talking to Ernesto. I take the last two steps up the path and stop for introductions, knowing for a fact that this man is not our eight thirty appointment.

"Vera," says Ernesto, "I would like you to meet a very old friend of mine. This is Leonard Cook. He's a doctor of energetic medicine. I asked him to drop by this morning to talk to you." I shake hands with Leonard—his hand is big and warm, the expression on his face open and inquisitive. I look from Leonard to Ernesto, feeling pleased with their mutual male attention.

"Come on in, Leonard," says Ernesto. His tightly muscled ass could not look any better if it tried. He stops next to the kitchen counter. "How about a cup of coffee?"

Leonard waits for me to walk in ahead of him as he says, "I'd love one." We congregate at the stove as Leonard accepts a mug from Ernesto. He holds the hot cup with both hands and takes a look around the cozy room. The lamps are all on and exude a warm light. The fire is lit. His eyes stop to rest on the little statue of White Tara sitting on the mantle above the fireplace. There is a fresh unlit candle in the glass holder sitting next to her.

He takes his first sip and walks toward the goddess. He stops in front of her and turns to Ernesto. "Who brought her here?"

"I didn't," Ernesto says as he looks at me. "Vera brought her here."

The silver of Leonard's belt buckle catches the firelight as he turns back toward me and asks, "Why?"

"I found her at a bookstore in the city—Polk Gulch Books on Polk? It was like I got tractor beamed into the place. Saw her, fell in love, bought her. There was something about her that made me need to have her here. I need—evidently—to learn about compassion."

"Really?" Leonard looks at me with increased interest. My heart warms—I like him already.

"Yes. I've been lighting candles for her ever since. I keep catching her smiling at me out of the corner of my eye," I say, and add, "I'm not joking."

"You don't need me then," says Leonard as he walks back over to the kitchen counter, setting his coffee cup down. "Ernesto told me you were looking for a mentor. But you seem to have already found your medicine. Just keep leaning into White Tara's lineage of compassion for support. If you call on her, she will help you. Do you know her mantra?"

"No."

"*Om Tare Tu Tare Tu Re So Ha,*" says Leonard. "Repeat after me."

"*Om Tare Tu Tare Tu Re So Ha.*" As I say the words, they feel strangely familiar in my mouth.

"Say it again a few times in a row. I want you to get used to the repetitive action of the seed syllables on your tongue."

I follow his command, feeling like I am trying to say, "She sells seashells by the seashore." My tongue falters over the sounds on the second round, turning them to garble. "I need to get the hang of this," I say, embarrassed.

Leonard says, "Don't worry. Mantra takes some practice."

"I like the sound, no clue why."

"Trust that. Start using it. Each time you use the mantra, you're calling on Tara to help and protect you." Leonard pulls a cell phone out of his pocket. He looks at it and says, "Unfortunately, I've got to go check in with another client. It's been a pleasure to meet you, Vera."

With genuine gratitude, I shake his hand, "Thank you. Nobody has ever suggested that I use a mantra for protection. I'll try it. I really appreciate your time."

"Here's my card. If you still find yourself needing assistance, give me a call." He pulls a simple white card from his breast pocket and hands it to me. I look at it briefly, catching something about tinctures and energetic medicine.

As I watch Leonard follow Ernesto out the door, I can hear Ernesto say, "Let me walk you out so we can catch up." The sound of their footsteps fades as they walk single file down the walkway.

Armed with the box of matches from the kitchen counter, I turn back to look at White Tara, murmuring her mantra softly. I walk over and light the waiting votive candle sitting next to her.

"What do you think?" Ernesto asks when he walks back in the door, closing it behind him. He looks bright-eyed, feeling proud of himself.

"Thank you for setting that up. I really appreciate it."

"I thought he would be a good resource for you. He's amazing when it comes to energetic medicine. You might consider treating yourself to an appointment. Self-care is essential in this kind of work. Or really any work. You always learn things when you watch other people work."

I've never had someone believe in me before. Not like this. All I want to do is kiss him. I am about to take the two steps that are left between us when we both hear footsteps coming up the pathway. In tandem, we turn to see that our eight-thirty has arrived.

CHERRI

12

A young blond woman, looking like a model for Free People, walks up the path. She wears an indigo flowered kimono over faded high-waist jeans. She walks up onto the porch barefoot and beautiful and enters the studio.

A gold ring pierces her septum. "Hi, I'm Cherri Blossom," she says as she offers me her hand. She leaves a strange scent behind her, one that I can't quite identify. The kimono billows behind her as she floats toward Ernesto, wrapping her arms around him in a lingering embrace. A repeat client of his, she clearly knows her way around.

He disentangles himself as she lets the kimono slip off her shoulders—it falls like a river, onto the floor. She pops the top button on her jeans and pulls the rest of the buttons apart using both hands as Ernesto walks toward me.

He opens the door and waits for me to go first before closing it behind us. We stand shoulder to shoulder on the porch keeping our backs to the windows. "That was quite an entrance," I say under my breath. He is about to answer when we hear the door open.

Cherri's voice interrupts, "I'm ready when you are."

In unison, we turn back to find Venus di Milo standing in the doorway, buck naked with her hip cocked. A tattoo of a pale pink lotus hovers delicately directly above her naked pussy lips. "I brought you what you asked for," she says as she holds out her right hand. In it rests a small blue glass bottle glittering in the dappled sunlight.

All business suddenly, he walks over and takes the bottle out of her hand. He slips it into the pocket of his athletic pants, making the bottle disappear.

"What's in the remedy?" I ask.

Cherri says, "Remedy? Perfect. It's the purest LSD around. Right, Ernesto? I like microdosing LSD while getting work. Next maybe some psilocybin." She pronounces this last word carefully like the chosen oracle for therapeutic use of psychedelics.

I roll my eyes at him   *Really?* You just have to be kidding me! LSD? A dash of psilocybin? What is this, the cooking channel? Until now, I've been clueless that he actually works like this. Sneaky bastard.

She turns to sashay her luminous bottom back in the direction of the table. My eyes continue to follow the curvature of the other side of her moon as he says, "Let me give you a brief synopsis of our work together. Our work today is to integrate Cherri's use of ayahuasca."

He remains impassive as she climbs onto the table, assumes the lotus position, and proclaims, "Ayahuasca is a plant-based psychotropic substance. I am using it regularly in circle as a way of remembering. I am also working with a medicine man. We've been using body-based work to integrate the intensity of its ongoing effects."

"He is called a *curandero*," he affirms.

As my impatience grows, White Tara catches my eye. The candle in the small glass holder sitting next to her fizzles out. The one I just lit must have been a dud. I grab another from a bag in the drawer of the desk and light it. When I return to the foot of the table, I take a deep breath and bend my knees slightly in quest of what is now that elusive thing called neutrality. How can I feel compassionate when I'm accumulating at least fifty opinions about this woman, her drugs, her fucking *curandero*?

"After I got home from a festival in Sri Lanka, I left for another ten-day intensive. I got back late Sunday night. This time I was working with the *curandero* one-on-one on an open platform. He left me for hours at a time so I could connect with Jaguar. Jaguar is my totem. I feel completely raw. It is so amazing. I still feel actually quite high," says Cherri.

Now as I catch another whiff of that funky smell, I realize she is literally off-gassing ayahuasca. Ernesto wheels the massage stool over to the right side of the table and sits down. "So how can we best serve you today?"

By way of an explanation, Cherri cups the underside of her breasts with both of her hands. "My boobs feel really sore and tight. Like it's hard to even raise my arms over my head. I've had this feeling off and on since I got them done, but the soreness really kicked in on that platform last week." When she is finished talking, she releases them and snuggles down into the sheets like a little girl.

Ernesto lays his right hand atop her breastplate over what he tells us is her manubrium, a bone roughly equidistant between the base of her neck and the beginning of her cleavage. As he does so, she yanks back the sheet to reveal her double c's one more time.

"What do you think?" Her question is directed at me.

I walk between the fireplace and the left side of the table and discreetly pull the flannel sheet back up over her breasts. "Nice," I say, feeling almost nauseated.

I sneak a look at the digital clock on the oven. The blue numbers read 9:33 a.m. We are thirty minutes into the session, but it feels like we have been here for hours.

"It's still hard for me to lift my right arm, like it's tight or restricted or something. But after that night out on the platform, the pain really kicked in."

I return to my spot at the foot of the table. The right side of my body from above my armpit all the way down along the inside of my arm, to the end of my right thumb feels like concrete. I stick my thumbs into my armpits. My elbows bow out as I grab ahold of the flesh to release the pressure.

Ernesto stands up unexpectedly. "See these two points here?" He points to two spots right above her armpits. "Vera, can you come around and work in this area. I need to use the WC."

I move to the head of the table and take over. Softly, I massage the areas where he left off.

All of a sudden, Cherri looks up at me. "Your energy is so different—oh, that feels amazing, Vera."

Startled, I take in the compliment, feeling shy. "How so?" I ask, assuming she is talking about my style verses Ernesto's.

"Hey, how do you know where things are stuck in my body anyway?"

"What do you mean?"

"You've been touching the places on my body where I feel the most stuck."

"The man-shaman says I transmute."

"You do what?"

"Transmute. It means I can feel emotions in your body with my body. Places that feel stuck and congested in you, feel stuck and congested in me—at least it works like that at times."

Cherri says sweetly, "Hey, I feel like I do this, too. I just don't know how I do it or even how to do it, I mean transmute. That's what you call it?" She looks up at me, waiting for a response.

"Everyone transmutes to one degree or another, but people just aren't usually aware that they are doing it."

For the first time, I realize I am actually doing client work at a different level. Cherri has just given me an opportunity to explain something about the body that might seem out there but isn't. I mean, if I really think about it, why wouldn't all our feelings be connected to one degree or another? Her attention gives me an idea. "Hey, I'm thinking of putting a group together to teach women how to—"

"Compost." The sound of Ernesto's footsteps come to a halt next to me on my left. "Can I have my chair back now please?" he asks. As I get up, I watch her expression of discovery shift in his direction. Demoted, I resume my position at the foot of the table.

What a bastard, I think. The realization comes with a *whoosh*. He then abruptly changes the subject. "We still haven't heard about what happened on the platform."

"Oh, right. So I did ceremony work for several days in a row with this *curandero* named Miguel. I mean, why travel all the way to Peru if I'm not going to go for it? I did a ton of medicine. Part of my initiation was to stay out on that platform by myself. I thought the whole thing was going to be so peaceful, like I was going to drop into some kind of synchronicity with the jungle and the universe. But it wasn't like that at all. Mostly, I was just scared shitless until Miguel finally came back."

"Then what happened?"

"I told him I felt like I'd done way too much. But he said my experience was totally normal. That I was just releasing old fear and not to overthink it."

"Does this resonate with you?"

"I mean, he's the medicine man. Everyone says he's like a guru when it comes to ceremony. It is considered a total honor to even be able to work with him. He's booked solid for months. That's why I flew down there."

"So how do you feel about what happened out on that platform right now?"

Suddenly childlike, her face caves in. "I feel like he abandoned me." She wraps her long pale arms around Ernesto's neck and wails. He holds her as she sobs, he comforts her.

More of the same until the session is over. After she gets dressed and they go outside, I remain inside to strip the table and put on fresh sheets. I can hear her rebook with him, and then she hugs him good-bye. She turns and waves at me before she walks back down the pathway.

I walk outside. "Why did you do that?" I ask.

"Do what?"

"Why did you disrupt my connection with her?"

"What do you mean?"

"I mean she was asking me a question about transmuting. Something I'm sure tons of women know how to do, but don't actually know they know how to do. We were having a moment. Then you interrupted it. Why?"

"We had other things to do, Tex. It was time to move on."

"Like integrate ayahuasca?" I roll my eyes so hard it's questionable whether my sensory organs for sight will ever recover. "Did you even consider that while she's trying to find out who she is in relation to herself, simultaneously she's overextending?"

I hold up my right hand and extend my index finger vertically. "She just got breast implants." I add my middle finger to the mix to make a peace sign. "Then she dashed to South America and did way too much ayahuasca out on some platform in the middle of butt-fuck-jungle-nowhere because she wanted to please the *curandero*."

I include my ring finger to make the number three. "Now she's bringing you whatever she thinks you want to please you. Don't you find number three just a little problematic given the nature of numbers one and two?"

INDIA

Ernesto's eyes hold mine for a moment before we turn to see our next client arrive, but we'll never find time to finish discussing our disagreement. The rest of the day's work is pretty simple and straightforward. I learn a lot of technical stuff from him, stuff that he is good at. He unravels an Achilles tendon for one woman and works on sciatica for another. The last session involves some deep work on a man's right shin for severe tendonitis.

When I get into my car, I've got a few texts. I'm surprised to find that the first one is from Cherri. She sounds flustered. As I read on, I realize that she wants to work with me. Solo. I read it twice, wanting to make sure that I fully understand her request.

She appears to have had some sort of meltdown since this morning. If I understand her correctly, she feels like she needs mentoring, a woman she can trust.

I have never worked with a client in this way before. I call her back immediately and leave a message thanking her for her interest in my work. I also explain that I will be out of town at the Esalen Institute through the upcoming weekend. I add that, if we are unable to connect by phone, I will send some appointment times via text. I wish her well and hang up, feeling buoyed up, ecstatic, like my professional life might be finally taking off.

I am also super excited about my upcoming class at Esalen. Located in Big Sur, the Esalen Institute is famous for its massage school, as well as for its extraordinary variety of workshops. Practitioners teach Esalen-style massage all over the world. I've been saving up to take a course there for a very long time.

I drive to Whole Paycheck to buy provisions for India. Living with her is like living with a linebacker in a slim and leggy female body, which means I spend an inordinate amount of time and money buying food. Apart from pizza, I am also often accused of never buying anything that is ready to eat. I therefore amass a pound of sliced ham, smoked turkey, a large baguette, butter, cheese, a jar of Claussen pickles, and a large bag of BBQ potato chips, ready-made and starving-user-friendly.

When I collect Francisco on my way back, he almost yanks my arm out of my socket in his bid for freedom. We merge onto the 101 and head for home.

India is sitting at the kitchen table with her computer when Francisco and I walk in the door. "How was the bus?" I ask as I walk into the kitchen.

"You are not going to believe it. On my way home, this kid with serious zits lights up a J in the back of the bus. The bus driver stops the bus in the middle of California Street and opens the doors. She gets up, walks back, and points at him. 'No one but no one smokes weed on *my* bus. Now get the hell off here.' And she just stands there with her hands on her hips till this skinny kid scampers off her bus. OMG! So many whiteheads, I really felt for him."

"And that was it?" I say as I dump my bags onto the wedging table.

"Yeah." India gets up and noses through the booty, strokes my head, and says, "Good Mama." I glow with maternal victory as I watch her tear into the bread package, take a piece, and marry it with a slice of ham. She returns to the table, munching.

"I don't know about you—I'm starving too. I thought we could eat now. Then you can take some of this with you on your freshman retreat," I say as I lay everything out on the table.

India is leaving tomorrow for four days of trust-building exercises with her freshman class. "Aren't you supposed to be rappelling off some rock or something?"

"It's gonna be so fun. Everyone says it's the best thing that happens this year."

"Because of the trust-building exercises?"

"No way, Mom. More like hooking-up exercises. It's supposed to be a huge hookup. Even bigger than formal."

"Are you trying to get a rise out of me?"

"Just wanted to see if you're paying attention."

"Yes, I am, and according to the emails, this retreat is very well supervised; apparently even a discussion of the coronavirus has been scheduled," I say as I join her with sliced tomatoes drizzled in olive oil.

"Mom, everyone is talking about this. *Everybody.* Everyone except for you," India says.

"Not really. Not everyone is obsessed with science. One of Ernesto's clients called me. She feels like she needs mentoring. Just the two of us."

"You mean Ernesto too?"

"No. It's pretty wild. Without him."

"WTF. That is definitely going to go over big."

"Why do you dislike him so much? He introduced me to a doctor of energetic medicine this morning. We are getting along super well, actually."

"Well, it's so true. *Ernest* is so not going to be into it. You have to know this about him, don't you?"

"Sweetie, I think you are underestimating him. Plus you are supposed to be nice to the woman who goes to work so she can buy your dinner. And he *is* my boss and mentor."

"My point exactly," says India.

After we finish cleaning up, I go into my bedroom and take a look around. It was Dad's room before it became mine, and not too much about it is any different than it was in my childhood. I even sleep in the same old bed—the one I may have been conceived in.

I go over to stand in front of the oak dresser with the matching mirror that sits on the wall across from my dad's queen-sized bed. I pull out a couple pairs of leggings with a few tanks and toss them into a bag. My fav jeans with the busted knees go in too as I think over the text from Cherri.

I am so grateful for this new opportunity that spontaneously I decide to call Ernesto and thank him. As I pick up my cell, however, I feel a faint brush or whisper on the back of my neck. I pause for a moment, cell in hand, and question whether telling him, as India might say, is a good idea.

Still, he is my teacher, so my first and natural inclination is to say, "Thank you, Master." Eager for his praise, I brush my instincts aside and call. After he answers the phone, I tell him my good news. When his response is silence, I begin to mentally flagellate myself—but not because I have chosen to disregard my premonition.

No, now I feel guilty because Cherri called me instead of him. I know this is totally codependent, but I just can't help myself.

The man-shaman asks, "You have a professional meeting with her, instead of me?"

Rather than being proud of me, he sounds incredulous.

I start backpedaling rapidly. "Well, as you know, I have a really great teacher." Just like that, I give him the spotlight and dilute my success. I continue to chatter nervously until we disconnect. When I hang up, I'm completely overwhelmed with anxiety.

I walk down the hallway toward the kitchen to knock on my former bedroom door. When I open India's door, I am aware that, like the rest of the house, not much has changed. This used to be my room. The walls are white. The same faded-red Mexican dresser stands against the same wall. The same old mirror hangs over it. India still likes the Victorian metal bed frame. She and Francisco look up at me from her rumpled bed with curious looks of expectation.

"You were right," I say. "He's not into it."

14

I wake up early the next morning and lie in bed feeling torn. On the one hand, I understand that Cherri was originally Ernesto's client. On the other hand, it's a free country. She is allowed to hire whomever she wants. Before vacating my bed, I decide that I am not going to let his lack of support interfere with my weekend.

I slide on some jeans and pull my hair back in a ponytail. I walk into India's bedroom. Francisco is lying on the bed, looking solemn.

"You all packed, sweetie?"

"I've got everything but my sleeping bag. Can you get it for me, Mom?"

"Sure, honey." I walk out into the hallway to a linen closet that serves as a repository for just about whatever we can squeeze into it. I pull out an old blue flannel sleeping bag. I wait for the avalanche of detritus I swear I am going to get rid of to come tumbling after it. The mess holds while I grab another sleeping bag for myself. I pull on my leather jacket and call it good. It's Esalen. Everyone goes there to spend most of their time flirting in the baths. We go there to be *naked*.

After breakfast, we carry our gear out to the car to pack up together. India puts Francisco on the back seat before she gets in.

As I pull out of our little dead-end street, I ask, "Still excited?"

"Yes. I even woke up before my alarm."

"That qualifies as very excited. You never do that."

"How about you? Are you excited about your class?"

"My class is about the gut. Should be interesting. But mostly I'm excited about those baths. I can use a good soak in the tubs. We're all going to have a good time. Even Frank."

India turns around to look at our mutt wedged between duffle bags in the back seat and asks, "What do you think, Francisco? Looking forward to your dogcation?"

"What'd he say?"

"He wagged his tail and smiled. He probably thinks we are all going camping or something."

"He's not going to be happy about this, even though he'll have a good time—my spies tell me he always does."

"I know. I'm not gonna sleep for three nights in a row," India says happily. She grabs her backpack and sleeping bag out of the backseat as I pull up in front of Fairview Prep. She hops out, gives us a quick wave, and is gone.

Next, I drop Francisco off for his dogcation in Marin before heading back over the bridge through Golden Gate Park. I turn off 280 toward the coast, taking the scenic route along Highway One.

As I wind around these curves, my mind wanders back to the conversation I had with Ernesto the night before. It is on this stretch of road that I realize it isn't my job to make myself smaller in relation to him or to anyone else, for that matter. His feelings in response to my success are just that: his feelings. Still, I keep driving, feeling impatient with the man's lack of support. As a result, I spend more time focused on him and what he isn't doing for my professional growth than I do on the big life-quake question: *Why was I so quick to negate my own success?*

Two and a half hours later, I drop down the breathtaking driveway into the Esalen Institute. I'm looking forward to treating myself to a massage delivered by someone who knows exactly what he is doing. And at the risk of sounding like—well, Grace—I do want it to be a man.

I park and walk into the front office to book my massage appointment. I am standing at the counter, cruising over the list of practitioners, when the man behind the desk says, "You should get a session with that guy."

He points to a man standing to my right. I turn and nearly fall over. I take in a gorgeous man, skin dark. Wearing a white T-shirt with a pair of loose pants and orange Nikes, he is a big guy about my age, with short black hair. And as the fates would have it, I already know him.

I actually had a massage with this man some months back, on one of my rare reprieves from parenting. As we glance at one another, I can tell that he doesn't remember me. I am enjoying my anonymity anyway. But he definitely is the same guy—Will—and the fact that he is now standing in front of me seems somehow predestined. He has an opening in forty-five minutes, so I book another—as it turns out—massage with Will.

I flashback to my first massage with him after a bad breakup with my last boyfriend and not long before I met Ernesto. I'd taken an overnight to Esalen to unwind. At eight in the morning, the only available massage time, I sat on a bench in the baths anticipating something soothing.

I was feeling pretty tender when Will collected me. I had followed him upstairs to an empty room where he showed me the table. After he left, I lay face down. I put my head in the face cradle, the padded attachment at the front of the table, waiting.

When he came back, he pulled back the sheet and put his big hands on my back. The heat emanating from his palms penetrated layers of soreness in muscles that I didn't even know I had. I was just beginning to relax when I heard Will say, "If I'm gonna finish this massage, you have gotta let go."

I didn't have a clue what he was talking about. Confused, I raised my head out of the cradle and looked over at my right side. I was horrified when I saw my hand was clutching his. I realized that when his big hand touched mine, I'd clung to it like a life raft, and this was all it took. I burst into tears.

I was so embarrassed—I'd go so far as to say ashamed—about having held his hand like a little girl. I couldn't have stopped crying even if I'd wanted to. Adrift, I cried all the tears for all the myriad times I had ever felt rejected.

Will pulled my head out of the cradle and turned me over. He grabbed a box of tissues. Then he climbed onto the table behind me and pulled me up onto his chest. There was no conversation. He didn't try to be a hero. He didn't try to analyze me; he didn't try to fix me. He was simply a practical man without an agenda who let me cry until my time was up. Then he handed me his card and said, "Give me a call if you want more work." I wanted to, but I never did.

Now here he is again, as if it is destiny. I walk down to the baths, ready for anything. This time I am confident that whatever is coming my way is going to be good. I undress in the concrete communal dressing area, hang my clothes on a peg and wind a large maroon towel around my naked body. I sit down on that same wooden bench to wait.

When Will walks in, he curls his finger in my direction, "Come with me, missy." He has an accent that I can't quite place. I follow him and ask, "Where are you from?"

"Jersey. Why?"

"Just wondering about your accent."

Over his shoulder he whispers, "Lived a lotta places. Been around."

I look at the tight curvature of his ass and feel quite sure that he has.

We arrive at a massage table sandwiched between two other tables occupied by clients and their practitioners. As I climb onto the waiting surface, the sound of running water fills the concrete room. Sunlight reflects off the Pacific Ocean below us and bathes me with light as I lie down on the table, faceup.

"What can I do for you today?" asks Will. I look up into brown eyes whose whites are preternaturally bright. Is it my imagination, or is this guy flirting with me?

This time I fess up. "I'm a massage practitioner. I could use some work on my hands and right forearm in particular, please. My ankles feel congested. The rest I leave to you."

He places two hot hands over my skin right above my heart. My body jolts slightly in response to his touch.

He nods in appreciation. "It would appear that you are alive." I jolt again. I look back up at him before closing my eyes. He is definitely flirting with me.

Will and I proceed to go on a very noisy and wild ride. This time, he drives my body like a Ferrari, pulling moves out of his hat faster than I can anticipate them. There is nothing rote about his work. Like some crazy carnival ride, I never really know where he is going to go next, so much so that I start laughing.

This is exactly what I need, but apparently our neighbors don't agree. When we hear someone *shush* us, not once but twice, Will jumps up onto the table with a huge shit-eating grin on his face, squats with his Nikes on either side of my hips, lays a big index finger against my lips, and says, "Hush now."

I am tempted to kiss that finger before he grabs a thigh and cat stretches me left, cat stretches me right. The look on his face is so mischievous that I only laugh harder. I mean, it's just so damn difficult to be spiritual sometimes, especially when I'm being manhandled.

Laughing is also undeniably liberating. I know I am releasing the stress that I've been holding about Ernesto's obvious problem with my professional growth. Plus, I'm laughing at the ridiculous corner I've backed myself into without even realizing it. Like why am I in a relationship with a married man who is also my work partner? These are questions surely worth laughing at.

So I do. Every time Will manipulates my limbs, my body vibrates in response. By the time he has finished dismantling my lower extremities, the massage has become nothing short of a revelation. I like this guy, and I can tell he likes me too. What he may lack in finesse, he makes up for with enthusiasm.

When we are done, I get off the table. Glowing, I wrap myself in a sheet and follow the vee of Will's broad shoulders narrowing to his waist back to the dressing area. Like any good athlete he is nimble.

"Thank you," I whisper when we get to the dressing area. "I haven't laughed that hard in a long time. Literally, I couldn't stop."

"I have a feeling I am going to hear about this one in our next Massage Crew meeting."

"You were all over the place. I loved those Thai moves. One more of those and I was going to fly off the table."

"No one flies off the table on my watch, baby. Listen, I would love to trade with you. I'm leaving for Monterey when I'm done here. I won't be back until Sunday afternoon. How long are you around?"

"I'm leaving Saturday morning."

He pulls a card out of a pocket and hands it to me for a second time. I look down at the card stock and read WILL CARVER: MASSAGE, his cell phone number below.

"Come anytime. We can spend the day together. Where do you live?"

"In San Francisco."

"I need to get up to the Bay. I'll text before my next trip. Thanks. Gotta run, girl." He catches me up in a huge and sexy hug and leaves. We've both just blown every professional boundary when it comes to a massage. But as Grace says, we are consenting adults.

I rinse off first in the communal shower area before walking outside to the baths, where I wade into the farthest tub. It is perched high above the ocean. I settle my back against the rocks. In some ways, laughing with Will was no different than bawling my eyes out. Either way, I feel free, as if I'm *changed*. There is no question that laughing with Will has been a lot more fun than crying with him, and now I feel emboldened as I close my eyes and tilt my face up toward the sun.

15
CHERRI

As it turns out, my second massage with Will is the juiciest part of my time at Esalen. I eat an inordinate amount of kale, spend a lot of time bathing, and take two long, deep, truly excellent naps, all of which I very badly need. The workshop itself is OK. So as I drive home on Saturday morning, I find myself missing the man of the hour, Ernesto, my love, my work partner, the bane of my existence.

Three hours later, I pull up in front of Fairview Prep to wait for India's bus to arrive from Shasta. When it does, the door opens to reveal a bunch of ragged, exhausted-looking teenagers. India walks over, chucks her dirty pack and sleeping bag into the back, and gets in.

"Sorry to break it to you, but we still need to pick up Frank."

"Mom, you cannot be serious? I need a shower so bad."

"I'll make it up to you. Just sleep in the car. I promise to cook something remarkable for dinner, like your favorite take out.I head over the Golden Gate bridge toward Marin as she groans from the passenger seat before falling asleep. Twenty minutes later, I spring Francisco from dog care and drive my filthy little family home.

As we pull up, I receive a text from Ernesto: I MISS YOU FREE AT 4PM FOR A CHAT?

Am I? I miss talking to him, I think. I text YES. At four o'clock, excited, I answer my cell.

"Texxx." He draws out the *x* luxuriously. I feel the sound of his voice in the floor of my belly. I don't really know how to describe it, but there is something about the quality or the authority of its tone that really turns me on. "How are you?"

"I feel really good," I say. "I had no idea how much I needed that. Plus, I got an excellent massage."

"Anybody I should know about?"

"His name his Will Carver. He's good, and he wants to trade."

"I'm sure he does."

"Don't undermine the compliment. There was some of that, but mostly it just made me miss your finesse."

"I can't wait to see you, baby."

I feel myself flush. "Any news?"

"Not really. I worked and then drove home. The place is cleaned up and ready to go for your client work in the morning."

"Great. I'm booked with Cherri first thing. Anything I should know about her?"

I steel myself as I listen to him thinking on the other end of the line. Then surprisingly, he says, "I'm happy that she wants to work with you. Yes, you should know that her parents are loaded, she has no boundaries, she's needy and requires lots of reparenting."

"I pretty much figured that part out, but thanks for the show of support. And Ernesto"—I can't believe I'm about to say this—"I really do care about you." This is the first time I've said anything like this out loud.

"We're good, baby. Don't worry. Gotta go."

I arrive early at the studio the following Sunday morning for my ten o'clock with Cherri. I crank up the heat before changing. I strap on my ankle bands and walk barefoot back into the main room to build a fire in the fireplace.

Next, I light a candle next to White Tara. I say her mantra repeating, *"Om Tare Tu Tare Tu Re So Ha"* a few times and call it good.

My cell dings behind me. When I walk over to the kitchen counter to check it out, I see the text is from Cherri.

10ISH MIN LATE

More than twenty minutes later, Cherri opens the door and gives me a long-armed hug, still wafting fumes from ayahuasca. She says, "I'm totally spun out," into my neck.

I disentangle myself and say, "Really? Why don't you get on the table? It's warm. Lie face up. I'll give you a minute to undress before I come back."

She established in that last session that privacy isn't something she craves, yet purposefully I close the door behind me. I wait with my back to the windows for her to undress and position herself on the table.

"I'm ready," she says, sounding like a little girl waiting for her bedtime story. When I return, I sit down on the massage stool, just like Ernesto, next to Cherri on her left side.

I slow my breathing down. It's an old bodyworker trick. In theory, her breathing should begin to entrain—this means sync up with mine—as I ask, "Tell me what's going on?"

It doesn't work. She blurts, "I almost got busted!"

"Busted how?"

"I had a bunch of chocolate psilocybin edibles in my car from my alchemist in Oakland. Coconut-based, totally vegan, organic, and locally sourced whenever possible, he makes them while chanting and only during certain phases of the moon.

Anyway, I was already in a hurry. I didn't want them to melt in the car when I got a text from my alchemist, you know."

She continues, "So I do the pick-up after our session last Monday. I'm on my way back to drop the edibles off at my girlfriend's house in Mill Valley when I almost run through the crosswalk in front of the

Whole Foods on Miller, with someone in it! You know the one I'm talking about?"

I know the crosswalk. Range Rovered victims of servitude scream through it on their way to touch up their highlights, or for some other equally imperative objective, so it is known as a life-threatening experience to the average pedestrian. I nod and keep listening.

Cherri continues. "I don't know what happened. I'm looking down at a text from my friend, look up, and there is this guy almost in front of me in the crosswalk. I hit the brakes. Thank god. But then I see flashing lights in my rearview mirror and realize I am getting pulled over by a motorcycle cop, with a car full of edibles. I am so fucked!"

I inhale deeply and exhale. "Well, it looks like you're still here. So what happened?"

"The cop gives me a moving violation! I have a small blue cooler on the backseat full of edibles, and I get a fucking moving violation! I say, 'Thank you very much, Officer' and drive away."

"Is this why you wanted me to work with you?"

"I mean, yeah. All this scared the shit out of me."

"Were you high?"

"No way. I never drive high when I'm transporting drugs. That would be completely stupid."

Oh well then, I think, *please forgive my stupid question.*

"Do you feel tired?" I ask. This question too is completely idiotic, but I want Cherri to be the one to discover that she must be exhausted. I mean, I am totally exhausted just listening to her.

"I was flying when I came in. Now I feel like I'm crashing."

No shit. I feel like I can barely move myself. "What does that feel like?" I ask.

"Like I'm on the backside of a huge caffeine and sugar buzz. Or crashing off too much substance. I feel jangly, totally wiped out."

'Jangly' is the perfect word for it. That jangly sensation is your nervous system saying, '*Stop it! Stop* fucking with me.'

"Let's take a break from talking for a little while. Why don't you turn over and lie down with your face in the cradle?" Mainly, I do this to give myself a break.

I hold the sheet up to give her privacy as she rolls over and plants her face in the cradle. Professionally, not to mention personally, I am in way over my head. I need a massage after just listening to her struggles. I wonder where the hell her parents are in all this.

And I do feel maternal as I lean over at the head of the table to place my hands on her very pretty back. Abruptly, she jerks her head up out of the cradle and head butts my forehead.

"I almost forgot to tell you. Ernesto and Star met with me last Friday. So you don't have to do that now—he'll be the one to work with me." She puts her head back in the cradle and wiggles down and in, getting comfy.

WTF? Forklift please! Needed to pry jaw off floor. I have no idea how he managed to swing it, but now, he is working with Cherri instead of me. Manipulative. Fucking. Bastard.

I am so furious I want to slug something; any available surface will do. This behavior, however, is unseemly from a professional point of view. *Massage practitioner goes nuts and trashes studio, kills random people* reads my psychic headline.

Instead, I bend my knees, drop my tailbone, and inhale into all the places where I feel blocked. I am blocked from head to toe. Every single chakra is saying *cerrado*. I focus on grounding my feet into the floor as my former enthusiasm about working with Cherri evaporates.

But being me, I hang in there. I mean what else am I going to do? Say, "Screw you" and "Ernesto, I'm dipping out." Oh, this sounds so tempting, but it wouldn't be kind.

Instead, I tap into this evolving thing called my mastery. I give her a simple detail and turn her over for the last fifteen minutes.

"Can you turn over for me?" I ask as I hold the sheet up again so she can roll upright.

I remove the face cradle and walk to the foot of the table. I grasp her ankles through the flannel sheet and pull downward to straighten the length of her body out, and then I set her feet down hip width apart.

I walk over to the kitchen sink to dampen a small towel with warm water. I walk back and wipe off the bottoms of her feet. Next I grab a roll of white surgical tape roughly two inches wide from the kitchen counter.

I ask, "Do you mind if I tape your feet?"

"Why? Sure, why not?"

"Just see how it feels, and then we can talk about it."

I wind the tape across the ball of Cherri's right foot and underneath and back across the top of her foot until I create a wide band. I use a pair of scissors to cut the tape. Then I repeat the same process with another heavier form of tan-colored surgical tape. I do the same thing on her left foot.

I walk to the head of the table. "Close your eyes, please. I am going to put an eye pillow over them," I say as I rest an eye pillow lightly over her closed eyes.

I select a small bottle of neroli oil from a collection of essential oils on the kitchen counter. I drop two drops of the oil into my palm, rub my hands together hard, walk over to open them, and wave the aroma of orange blossoms above Cherri's nostrils. I watch her as she inhales deeply.

"Oh, my god, that smells so good."

Neroli oil is an aphrodisiac. It also has the therapeutic quality of being an antidepressant. I spread the rest of the oil from my hands along the contours of Cherri's neck.

"I'm so glad. Now please focus your attention on your feet. Can you feel the tape?"

"Yes."

"How does it feel?"

"I feel more secure."

"Is that a good feeling?"

"Yes!" answers Cherri. She sounds like she's struck gold.

Finally! Let's see how long this discovery is going to last. At the risk of sounding cynical, my bet is inside of thirty-five minutes tops. I remove the eye pillow from Cherri's eyes and sit down on the massage stool next to her.

She opens her eyes and looks over at me with the first open expression I've seen on her face today. She looks all of twelve years old; her self-defense mechanism masquerading as bravado is gone.

My heart softens as I look back at her. I say, "It is an honor to work with you, Cherri. Why don't you lie here for a moment? Keep feeling the tape on your feet. When you're ready, stand up and walk around. Feel the sensation of your feet connected to the floor. Then get dressed and meet me out on the porch."

I walk outside and close the door behind me. When she joins me, she looks like a different woman. She says, "Oh, my god, I feel so much more grounded."

"Do you have any surgical tape at home?"

"No, why?"

I hand her the roll of tape. "Here, a present. Every time you want to feel more grounded and less fearful, try taping your feet. Self-love is a practice like anything else. All we have to do is to remember to *do* it."

Cherri takes cash out of her wallet, counts out $175 for the hour-and-a-half session, and hands it to me. She wipes her long thick bangs out of her eyes and stands up to give me a big girlish hug before turning to walk down the stairs. I watch her long blond hair move as her hips sway from side to side. She turns the corner before I pick up my cell.

I punch in Ernesto's number and listen to his cell roll over into voice mail. I leave a message saying, "Houston, we have a problem.

You have just undermined our partnership." I hang up and sit there for a moment, checking in with myself. More than anything, I feel incredibly tired. Then I strip the table for my next client.

JEAN

Shortly after my next session is finished, my cell ringtone chimes. It's him.

I pick up and say, "Hi."

"It isn't what you think."

"No?" I am monosyllabic.

"Really."

"Really? Tell me why not."

"The whole thing happened spontaneously."

"You mean you just happened to spontaneously be with Star and Cherri and then spontaneously had a session?"

"Yes and—"

"And you spontaneously didn't bother to tell me when we spoke on the phone? I would have thought this would have been the very first thing on your mind. You know how excited I was to have the opportunity to collaborate with her."

"I have a lot going on, Vera. It slipped my mind."

"You weren't even calendared with Cherri."

"I know, but she wanted another session, and that was how the whole thing unfolded."

"Last I heard, you were fully booked."

"You have to trust me, Tex. I had a cancellation. I have a proposal for you. Jean wants to come down tomorrow, Monday, overnight. She's been asked to lead a shamanism circle by a group from the East Bay. I know she plans to call you to ask if the T Room is free. Are you open to coming up the coast for the night so we can talk about this in person instead of on the phone?"

"Is everyone going to sit around this studio burning sage and beating drums under the full moon? I'm booked for a nine o'clock on Tuesday morning, a long one."

"You know I love your sarcasm. Would you mind rescheduling it, honey? You can still get to work. Or you can leave early."

"Do you want me to do this for you or for her?"

"This is about us, you and me."

I chew on that for a moment. I want to see the look on his face while we are having this conversation, so I relent. "My main concern is India. I need to see what plans I can make for her before I make any commitments."

"Jean's car just drove in the gate. I want to resolve this between us, baby, but I really have to run. Can you let me know sooner rather than later?"

"Why? So you can get some other woman to come up and fuck you instead?" I hang up feeling salty, though I actually would not put it past him. But Ernesto is right. We are not about to resolve this thing on the phone, which means if I can get India a sleepover at her best friend's house, I am actually willing to—depending on the traffic—drive the fucking hour plus up the coast.

When I get home later, I walk into India's room to find her still in bed with her computer. Leaning against a pile of pillows, she is curled up wearing flannel pajamas and with Francisco next to her. He opens one brown eye, wags his tail at me, and goes back to sleep.

I sit down on the edge of the bed. "Hi, do you have a minute?"

"Hi, Mama. Yeah. What's up?"

"I am having a problem with the man-sham, and I need to go up to see him. Do you mind if I drive up to have a conversation with him at his house tomorrow?"

"Jean is going to love that. Does she know about this?"

"She's coming down to Marin to lead a shamanism circle. She doesn't know."

"How convenient. What the fuck is a shamanism circle?"

"Don't swear," I say reflexively. Then I add, "Never mind. Fuck it. It's in our DNA.

"Shamanism? I don't know. Not my world. I guess people sit around beating drums and shaking rattles under a full moon or something. Your guess is as good as mine."

"Weird. So he did *what* to make you want to drive up there?"

I explain the situation. She listens patiently. When I am done, she says, "Well, your mentor obviously has a primitive need to compete with you. Doesn't sound like much of a mentor."

"Could you be any more sarcastic?"

"Mom, you know I'm not a fan. He's married, and now he's competing with you professionally, trying to keep you down, undercutting you. But I guess you could also interpret it as a compliment. And, no, I don't mind."

I haven't even articulated this last idea to myself. "Why the fuck do your synapses fire so much more quickly than mine do?"

"Don't swear, Mom," she says before she whispers, "It's called fucking evolution."

"I'm jealous. Would you mind sleeping over at Claire's tomorrow night?" She and Claire have known each other since kindergarten. Claire's mother is, I know, more than happy to host India and Frank on a school night.

Defiant, India looks back at me. "I am old enough to stay by myself." In some ways, her declaration comes as a relief. I mean she *is* old enough, isn't she? I was alone all the time by the time I was in high school, probably even in middle school. Parenting according to my dad fell into the wildly inappropriate category. India's childhood has only been moderately inappropriate by comparison. And most of that is fairly recent, within the past few months since Ernesto showed up.

I cave. "OK. But we need to drop Frank at that daycare place on Lombard tomorrow morning, and you will need to pick him up on the way home from school."

"Cool."

"Life is always so easy with you, honey. I don't know why I am so blessed as a mother, but I want you to know that I never ever take you for granted," I say as I walk out into the hallway toward the kitchen.

My daughter may be chronically exceptional, but all I feel is a kind of soul sickness as I head for the refrigerator. This is a feeling with which I am becoming increasingly familiar. I am now in the process of becoming accountable for certain choices I've made with regard to the man—to go global—with regard to every man I've ever been with.

What made me believe that Ernesto was going to treat me any differently than he treats his wife, Jean? What made me perpetuate this level of fantasy? What made me imagine that our connection is exempt from his capacity for betrayal? Have I—I wonder—been inventing him?

This inclination of mine to overlook his transgressions, to default into the implausible, is huge. After all, I want to look up to the man professionally. I want to come up with reasons for why he might have created that session. And even brought in Star. I even try to find a way to dismiss his behavior, but how can I when he literally sideswipes me?

India's voice breaks into my reverie. "Mom?"

"What?"

"You OK?"

"Not really. I feel shaky but will no doubt live. I always do. Do you have a lot of homework?"

"You can't help me with it anyway, it's so over your head. Also, could you just make sure to leave me a bunch of food, please?"

"Sure, baby." I'm so grateful that some things in my life never change; India, her awesome appetite. I am also relieved that I can be this honest. My relationship with a married man makes me no paradigm of maternal virtue, but the fact that we can be this transparent with each other is a gift.

I pull my cell out of my back pocket and text him: SEE YOU TOMORROW.

Then I grab a bag and head out on foot to forage for sustenance.

The next morning, Monday, is whacked from the get-go. First, I am awakened by a text from Ernesto: SHE IS LEAVING AT TEN O'CLOCK DRIVING BY WAY OF SIR FRANCIS DRAKE.

From there on out, the text flow is nonstop with updates on Jean's every ETD. Jean also—incredibly—phones, but I don't pick up. When they both call me simultaneously from their home line, I begin to feel completely suffocated.

Now I don't even feel like going anymore, which strikes me as a healthy response. But I said I would, so I pack a change of clothes in my daypack, along with a toothbrush. *Just in case*, I tell myself.

After a quick bowl of granola, I drag myself out to the car. India jumps in and puts Francisco on her lap. We head onto Lombard to drop off Frank. She deposits him at his daycare and gets back in. Next, I pull up in front of her school. She hangs back for a moment in the car. Briefly, she puts a delicate left hand on the newly busted-out hole of my black jeans' right knee.

"Good luck, Mom. I know you can do it."

"You have more faith in me than I do at the moment but thanks, honey. I really appreciate your support."

Then she's gone. Feeling sentimental again, I sit watching her make her way into school.

I head for the studio because it's a mess, my being so pissed and so tired after Cherri that I just hadn't felt like cleaning up yesterday. Now I need to organize it for Jean before I head north.

As I begin to cross the Golden Gate, my phone chimes at me yet again from the passenger seat. I look over at it and finally ask myself, "What the fuck am I doing?"

It's a drop-dead beautiful morning. I am driving over one of the most scenic bridges in the world, and both my lover and his wife are frantically texting me. What could possibly be wrong with this picture?

Suddenly, I feel so tired. When I eventually walk into the T Room, it feels like I'm in the eye of their entirely fucked-up marital maelstrom. I sit down at the desk and look up at a piece of yellow legal paper taped to the wall. I stuck it there at eye level yesterday. I read the words out loud:

"Competition is self-negating."

On the desk below my words of wisdom sits a card with a purple butterfly from the Amazon on the front. I pick it up and spin it around in my fingers, feeling meditative as I look at the dappled light streaming in through the window, covering my left arm.

I know writing a letter such as the one I am feeling tempted to write is crazy. I'm aware it goes against the laws or rules of the world in which I live. Yet I am astonished to realize that out of nowhere, I feel enormous gratitude. I mean, how often does a woman get the chance to be with a man in more than one lifetime. Not often enough, even if he *is* being a total dickhead.

I know by most people's standards, it's an experience that they are never, ever going to have. Maybe it isn't something they would even want to have. Because the truth is, this affair is complicated.

I pick up a pen.

I read the words on the wall again. I open the card and begin with the sober salutation:

"Dear Jean:"

I know it sounds crazy, but I thank her for the opportunity to grow. I write that I am heading to their house to tell her husband "we are done."

I sign off, "With love." Then I close the card and say a humble, "Amen."

I find a homemade blend of essential oil I've dubbed "Tranquility." Figuring we can all use a little assistance, I walk over to open a diffuser sitting on the kitchen counter. I fill it with a soothing mix of lemon myrtle, melissa, ylang ylang, and Hawaiian sandalwood. I leave the bottle—together with the card on the desk—with a Post-it, saying it's a gift.

I strip the table and remake it. I also put a fresh roll of toilet paper in the holder, because I'm nice. But when I look at myself in the mirror, I ask the woman looking back at me, "Am I really ready to be this bold?"

More accurately, am I really ready to leave this man and this studio? I'm not so sure, so I take the card back on my way out.

I turn left onto Shoreline/Highway One, toward Stinson Beach, feeling trapped as if I'm stuck in a groove. I know it's time to move on, but I'm clearly having a hard time with the moving on part as I take turns that circumnavigate Mt. Tam and make my way to the coast below.

It is outside Stinson that I notice a dead bird on the left-hand side. Its feathers blow in the chilly wind. I downshift, make a U-turn, and drive back to park on a small pullout, wondering if the bird might be a hawk.

I open my car door and pause. I feel that same faint whisper on my neck. Silently, I ask, "Could Jean be coming this way?"

My logic says, *Of course, not. After Ernesto's ten thousand texts, surely I would know. Right?*

I catch the thread of my anxiety. Concerns like these are robbing me of valuable parcels of my mental real estate.

Reminding myself to breathe, I walk over to the bird. It turns out to be a wild turkey. Finding a dead turkey in the road sounds like a setup for a joke. But on this Monday in January, it could be propitious. I Google the sucker.

"The turkey is called the Earth Eagle and is a totem of shared blessings and harvest."

It is actually a federal offense, I find, to harvest roadkill. I take my left boot, press it against the remains of the carcass, and try yanking out the feathers, which are stubborn. They hold. But I'm not taking *no* for an answer. With repeated tugging, slowly, one by one, the feathers begin to give.

Cars whoosh by as I walk back to the car with my handful of greasy feathers. I put them in the trunk, rinse my hands off with a bottle of water, wipe my still oily fingers on my black jeans, and get into the car. Feeling satisfied, I turn back up the coast.

I am just passing through Dog Town when my phone dings with a text. Thinking it must be from Ernesto, I pull over. To my surprise, the text is from Jean:

WAS THAT YOU PARKED IN A HURRY OR WOULD HAVE STOPPED TO SAY HELLO

I burst out laughing. After all the phone calls, a good-bye, I-am-becoming-a-butterfly card, and a bunch of turkey feathers, I run into his wife. Not only that, but she just texted to tell me so. This effectively means she sees me heading to her house. After all, that is where this road leads, and I have no other reason to be on it.

Her husband and I are *officially* busted. How fucking funny is that?

VERA

I lean back in my seat and look up out of my sunroof at the blue and limitless sky. This text is bait on the end of a karmic hook. If I respond with a lie, I am compromising myself. If I tell the truth, I engage in a dialogue that I don't want to have. I decide to do neither and throw my phone next to the card on the passenger seat next to the card. I drive up the coast, feeling like I am unwinding some old pattern instead.

I'm almost a hundred percent sure Jean knows all about our affair. What I can't understand is why she doesn't just keep up the ruse and pretend that she hasn't seen me, which would make it all so much easier. As I think it through, however, I realize that she is trying to corroborate the evidence. I mean, she wouldn't need verification if she trusted what she's seen, right? From my perspective, she is double-checking because she doesn't entirely trust her intuition.

Until yesterday, my initial response would have been to create a cover story. Like so many women, I am a fucking professional when it comes to holding other people's feelings. I've been socialized to perform for love and protection. I mean, just hold up the flaming hoop, and I'll dive on in naked sans sunscreen.

I have compassion for Jean's predicament. But, actually, it's her responsibility to have a truthful conversation with her husband, not mine. I pull over a little south of my destination onto the shoulder. I text an honest: HEY YES I AM ON A PILGRIMAGE.

The second part is a kind of random thing to say, but this drive up the coast feels like some form of one; it's just that this pilgrimage isn't one I yet fully understand.

My chore accomplished, I continue until I come to a stop in front of the gate. I wait for it to open as if magically before slowly driving along the gravel driveway to park my car across from his man-yurt.

In the rearview mirror I watch Ernesto emerge from his cave. Luna bounds toward me as he comes over to open my car door. Ever the gentleman, he pulls me out into his muscular arms, kissing me before picking me up bride-style and carrying me back over the threshold into his lair.

He puts me down in front of a wood-burning stove and says, "I made something for you." I consider interrupting him to tell him that his wife has just seen me on the road as I watch him pick up an old, hand-forged metal tool. He holds it vertically, displaying a large brass coin emblazoned with a Chinese character. The coin is laced with copper wire and welded onto the surface of the implement. He hands it to me. It is heavy as hell.

Immediately, I know what it is. A spear. I Googled somewhere in my recent research on White Tara that Tibetan Buddhists consider the point of the spear to symbolize the piercing or impaling of all false notions or distorted ideas. Now, here he is, giving the ideal gift to cut through my sense of limitation. Either that or I bonk the son of a bitch over the head with it and call it good. Suddenly, I feel like bawling as I spin the thing in my hands.

I restrain both urges as I say, "I have something to show you. Wait here. I'll be right back."

I heft my spear and take it with me as I walk back to my car. I yank out my backpack and make for the massage room, close the door, and strip. While I do so, I take a good look at myself in the mirror along the back wall. *Not so bad,* I tell myself as I wield my no-animal-cruelty eye pencil like a weapon.

Lining my green eyes in heavy charcoal gray, I smudge. Then I put the leather thong body jewelry around my hips and line the tiny brass flames up front to back. I look down at the flame in the front as it grazes the flame of closely shaved pubic hair just above my clit. I point my fanny toward the glass to survey the flame in the rear. It nestles nicely into the crack of my ass.

According to yogic terminology, each amulet now rests just above my first—or *muladhara*—chakra, the location that holds my sense of security. Or so they say.

Spear in hand, I walk barefoot back outside along the path toward my destiny. I enter the door. Shaman leans back against the counter with a glass of whiskey halfway to his lips.

"Jesus," he says not taking his eyes off me. He puts his glass down. "That thing looks so damn good on you, baby."

I don't answer. I don't feel like reminiscing.

He takes a step toward me. "What should I call you? Durga? Or is it Kali?"

Researching my own goddess, I've discovered that Durga and Kali are both goddesses too. Being compared to either or both works for me in a very big way right now.

I spin the spear in my right hand and command, "Stop." He freezes, relaxes, and leans back against the counter again as he picks up his glass. Clearly, he is enjoying my theater.

I turn a very slow 360 in front of him, just so he can eat a little more shit. Then I burst his bubble and say, "I didn't put this rig on to seduce you. I'll admit that the thought has crossed my mind. But not today.

"I put this thing on to show you something. You just called me Durga. She is a Hindu warrior goddess. She rides a tiger wielding seven different implements. They say her handy tools are designed to bust illusion."

Despite the warmth from the fire, I stop for a moment and shiver. "You're the one who made me this fucking chastity belt. So why do you keep getting me all dressed up for the party then leaving me with no place to go?"

I shiver again, harder this time. He takes off an old flannel shirt, paint splattered and battle weary. He crosses the distance between us to hand me the shirt.

"I am so sorry, Tex. I am sorry for all of it. But right now, I want you to know that not only did I make you that spear, but I am literally giving you the shirt off my back."

What a manipulative, bullshit scenario. My work partner snakes my meeting, I go see him to talk about it, and he gives me a hand-forged spear along with the shirt off his back. Please.

But my capacity for clarity is compromised. I'm involved, attached, and more than anything, confused. There are just too damn many ingredients in our mix.

Suddenly, I feel cold and tired. I therefore accept the shirt. As I pull it on, I can smell him. I nod to the whiskey. "Can I have some of that please?"

He pours me a large cut crystal glassfull from the bottle and hands it to me before wrapping a soft fleece blanket around my shoulders. Gently, he pushes me back into a chair. He sits down across from me, lifting my feet into his lap, and begins to massage away the chill that has settled in.

I take a sip and roll it around in my mouth. "Your wife saw me on the road."

He raises his eyebrows.

"You heard me right. There was a dead turkey. I stopped to collect the feathers."

"Of course, you did."

I can't help smiling. "She must have seen me. Either she saw me on the road, or she saw my car. By the time I got to Dog Town, she'd already texted asking if it was me."

"What'd you do?"

"I didn't do anything."

"What do you mean you didn't do anything? Why didn't you just text her back and create a diversion?"

"Why don't you call it what it is?"

"What do you mean?

"You know damn well what I mean."

"If you want to put it that way—then yes, Tex—I mean lie."

I take another sip of whiskey and say, "I don' wah-nah lie no mo."

"Are you quoting some ancient soothsayer from one of your past lives?"

"No. I'm quoting a mash-up I heard with Tina Turner telling Ike she's had enough. Don't tell me you—of all people—haven't heard it?"

"Have you had enough?"

"I'm tired of lying, Ernesto. Aren't you? Aren't you the one who taught me that lying takes the body out of integrity? According to our course work, the act of lying disrupts our natural capacity for somatic integration. And according to you, the body itself does not lie but merely interprets all the lies we inflict on it in ways that may result in dis-ease. That last sentence is a direct quote from you. Asking me to lie is like asking me to consciously hurt my own body. Remember all that?"

He's quiet for a few moments. "You've been a good student."

I lean toward him. "Thank you for noticing. I'm not being sarcastic. I take that as a huge compliment. But your decision not to tell me about taking that meeting undermines whatever foundation we might have had in our working partnership. Do you get it?"

He remains silent.

I stare at the powerful object that he has made me, standing in my hands. "What does the Chinese character mean on the coin?" I ask.

"It's the character for family."

I am oddly touched as he puts my feet down. Silently, he walks over to the counter and picks up the bottle to pour himself some more.

"How would you like some work on your neck?"

I pull my feet up underneath the blanket and sit cross-legged. Now that he mentions it, my neck hurts like hell. I move my head from side to side. As I dig the fingers of my right hand into the attachments at the base of my neck, I decide to take him up on his offer.

"I could use the work."

He walks over and unwraps the blanket from my shoulders before taking my hand to pull me up to a standing position. His other hand pushes my bottom forward, so I walk in front of him as the flannel shirt grazes my thighs.

VERA

He syncs his cell to an independent speaker on a shelf, Van Morrison singing "Peace of Mind."

"This a setup?" I ask.

He sings the chorus, "Because I'm just a man, oh I ain't got no plans . . . I'm just trying to find some peace of mind . . ."

"Keep me posted how that works out for you," I say as I divest myself of my regalia.

I climb onto the table and ask, "Why isn't what you already have enough?"

"How so?"

"Your professional life is so dynamic. It's inconceivable to me that my session with Cherri was really worth competing over. You even brought in Star. What's the matter with us, Ernesto?"

He remains silent. I assume that Ernesto is thinking about my question, so I give him some space as I lie there waiting to receive work on the right side of my neck. But come to think of it, he never does give me an answer. Instead, he leans over and kisses me, long and deep. For my part, I can't resist responding, and when he mounts me, I welcome it, hating myself.

Except when he enters me today, our sex hurts. Quickly, I do a vaginal survey—it's not a yeast thing—I have a PhD in yeast infections—and it isn't a bacterial thing, a UTI; I've had one of those, and this is different. I am stuck with only one other alternative. Grudgingly, I hate admitting that this pain could be an emotional thing, my body telling me to please stop.

His cum has always felt downright *good* for my pussy. In fact, my vagina has never felt better than it has with him, until right now. It seems like a stretch, but could it be possible that the discrepancy between the fantasy and the reality of our relationship is manifesting itself in physical symptoms?

I say, "Babe, I gotta stop."

"Why, honey?"

"My pussy hurts so much right now. It feels like you're rubbing me raw. I must have some kind of inflammation."

"Should I take this personally?"

"I don't know." I promise my pussy that I will check in with her later. This is a first. We always finish each other off. Awkward, we stand up. I drop the leather thong down around my ankles, step out of it, and pull my jeans and shirt back on.

Then I follow him out into the driveway where there are a bunch of broken boards lying around.

"What's all this?"

"It's the remains of the frame I originally made for our bed. I had to dismantle it to get it out of our bedroom."

"Why are you getting rid of it?"

"It's a bizarre story. You know the sliding glass doors we have in our bedroom?"

I nod. I've only been there once. I never had a desire to spend time in his and Jean's house, especially the bedroom, as something about it gives me the creeps.

He continues, "One of the doors fell off its track when we were in bed. The glass smashed into the bedframe and broke, shattered glass everywhere."

This sounds so unbelievably scary. "Seriously? Did this happen while you were sleeping? Were you both OK?"

"Yeah. It woke us up. We weren't hurt, but the frame was destroyed. I'm dismembering the rest of the wreckage for the fire," says Ernesto like that's it.

But there's something about this story that doesn't add up for me. I'm not sure what it is, but I ask, "So that's it?"

"What do you mean?"

Then it hits me. I blurt it out before I really even have time to know what exactly it is that I'm saying. "No shit. Of course, the glass fell off its track. You can't lie into and all around and about your marriage for years, be a healer, and not incur some of the universe's heat."

Ernesto picks up the hammer sitting on the ground next to him, keeping his head down. "I'm not having this conversation with you, Tex," he says as he starts pulling nails out of the fractured wood. "Anyway, she already bought a new bed online."

Oh, OK, so no fucking problem—I am incredulous. "Of course, she did. UPS regularly cycles through this driveway three times a day. Why would Jean ever deal with the nature of her reality when she can just buy more shit online?"

I'm really warming to my subject now, buying needless stuff. This happens to be one of my favorite pet peeves when I'm not out of my mind wasting money buying red porn bras from The Pink Pussycat.

"It's just too easy to buy shit these days. Nobody has to feel feelings anymore. Never mind the carbon energy expended to create stuff for more landfill." Defiantly, I cross my arms and wait for a response. When none is forthcoming, I decide to drop it. Instead, I set off for a solitary stroll toward an apple tree.

I have eaten and enjoyed an awful lot of its forbidden fruit. Just for good measure, I pluck a withered one before chucking it.

The depth of my lust has been reduced to the limitations of a power struggle. And I'm hungry. I walk back to my car to retrieve a canvas bag from behind the driver's seat. Inside is a loaf of bread and a pound of really good cheddar. I take the staff of my life into the massage room kitchen and am making a sandwich when Shaman walks in. He wraps the loaf of bread back up and sticks it in a bowl as he says, "It's almost five thirty. It's time for me to go wind things up."

This is code for time to call his wife, all part of the intricacy of their private algorithm. I keep my mouth full as I watch him pull a pan of lamb chops out of the fridge. The meat is studded with garlic, olive oil, red wine, and rosemary. He sets it down on the counter before he leaves for his man-yurt to make his call.

I sit down to read a quarterly issue of *Massage Magazine*. When he returns, he collects the pan and goes back outside. I can hear him start the fire in the barbeque as the smell of cooking meat starts to waft through the open door.

I get up to put out two plates side by side. I follow this ritual of coupledom with a pair of knives and forks, aware that this rite of intimacy is so much reliant on illusion.

So, OK, I do have a thing for the man who can cook. My father really knew his way around the kitchen. When Ernesto comes back inside, he says, "Sit." I climb onto a chair obediently as he serves me two small lamb chops encrusted with cumin before he fills my glass with a red pinot.

"I made you your favorite." And it is.

"I noticed."

"Do you like the rub, baby? I added a little more cumin this time."

"It's absolutely delicious," I say as I take another bite of the lamb and savor it. Slowly. He watches me swallow and puts a warm hand on my thigh, and I can feel myself getting wet one more time.

It's still dark when I leave early the following Tuesday morning. I drive along Highway One reflecting on the dualities of our relationship. On the one hand, for reasons beyond common sense, I have a profound physical weakness for this man. On the cusp of losing me, he's becoming more romantic and attentive than he has ever before been. From this narrow perspective, there is absolutely nothing about him not to like.

If, on the other hand, I have the courage to look more objectively at the whole picture of our relationship, our reality absolutely outweighs my fantasy. Ernesto is married. No one is going to give me an award for being with a married man. If anything, women in particular will be harder on me than on him—we expect one another to treat each other as sisters. Despite the fact that he is the one who has taken the oath of marital fidelity.

And my pussy now hurts when we make love. The insistent pain makes me keep asking myself—both during and after—could my participation in their marital lie be physically damaging my body?

But I've chosen not to make any hard or definitive decisions. Because I am afraid to leave him, I allow our predicament to remain unresolved. Short of dissolving our partnership, there isn't really anything more I can accomplish. I don't feel ready to claim my independence yet, and I still think I need his help.

But I need space too. I consider what not having sex with him might feel like the next time he is in Tam Junction. We could work, trade, and even see each other socially. I imagine that not sleeping with him could represent my initial step toward my individuation.

It doesn't take a degree in human sexuality to know that Ernesto will not be happy about this idea. I'm not all that sure I am either. I hate to admit it, but I still love the sound of his voice calling me "baby."

INDIA

S ome one-plus hours later, I park curbside in front of 5 Tennessee
Valley Road in Tam Junction. It's a very gray morning as I walk
through the gate, around to the back, and duck under the Santa Rosa
plum before taking the two steps up to the studio porch to slide my
key in the lock. But while the studio may look the same, something
about the place feels off. When I try to imagine what it could be, I
can't come up with a logical explanation. But something is definitely
different, even strange. It certainly feels damp; the fireplace stands
cold and empty.

I build a fire. I crank up the heat before getting a candle for White
Tara. I light it and sit back down on the massage chair to look up
at her benevolent smile. I repeat her mantra a few times under my
breath until the sound of footsteps on the pathway signals the arrival
of my first client.

Later that evening, I walk into our house feeling worn out. Given
her patience with my recent absences, I've decided to make India her
favorite: roast chicken, potatoes, and green beans. Later, I pull the
golden bird out of the oven. By the time we sit down at the table, I'm
feeling like a domestic goddess.

That is until India says, "I got a zero on my history essay."

"What?"

"The teacher didn't give us a reminder for the class assignment, and I missed getting it in on the online portal." Tears start to well in India's eyes.

"I'm sorry. It's so disappointing."

She bats away a tear. "It was shitty. I went in to talk to Mr. Wilkinson. He would not give me a break. He told me 'you are in high school now, India, this isn't middle school. This is what people will expect of you in the real world.' I told him that it is the first time I've ever missed handing in an assignment, and you know what he said?"

"What?" The ding of my cell intrudes into our conversation. I turn my phone over face down on the table.

"He said that I will never forget to hand in an assignment again."

"Brutal."

India nods. "I know, right? It just made me so angry. Three other kids missed the assignment too, and there is nothing any of us can do about it. It's ten percent of my grade. That means I have to get a hundred percent on everything else if I want to get an A-minus."

"What a task master. Will he let you do some extra credit?"

"Right now, he says no. He might see what the class average is toward the end of the semester, but he said it's unlikely."

She pushes her chair away from the table. "I'll be right back." While she is gone, I turn my phone over to check it. I read a text from Ernesto: IN TOWN UNEXPECTEDLY YOU FREE?

I respond: NO SPENDING MY EVENING WITH INDIA.

I turn the phone's sound off. It feels good to be sitting at the table waiting for India. I've missed her and devote the rest of our evening together to being this girl's mom.

When I wake up the following Tuesday morning, there is a text waiting for me from Star. It reads:

WHERE IS MY WHITE CLAW

The text was sent at 12:08 a.m. I reread the text. I close it and open the following text from Ernesto at 12:15 a.m. It reads:

WHITE CLAW 12 PACK MISSING FROM T ROOM? SUCH IS THE MYSTERY XXX

Assfuckinghole. I consider my options. My inbox fills with accusations hurled like burning embers sent from enemy terrain. The vitriolic stream of Star's consciousness flashes across my screen. As I will not deign to lower myself to this form of communication, I continue to include the sham-man on the thread.

I text him privately; it reads: WE NEED TO TALK.

We make a date for four o'clock. After my session ends, I jump into the shower and change into my civilian clothes. The tail-end of a fire is burning in the fireplace when Ernesto walks through the front door and drops a couple of things on the kitchen counter. The votive next to the statue of White Tara has guttered out.

He looks up at me as he begins stripping the table, standing up with an arm full of sheets. He has dark circles under his eyes and looks hungover.

"What is going on?" I ask.

"To be honest, I don't know myself."

"Would you like to try and explain it to me?"

"My dinner finished on the early side. I got a text from Star. She said she was in the neighborhood and asked if she could drop by.

"I figured, why not? It wasn't that late—around eight thirty—so I said 'sure,' imagining we would have a couple of drinks and do a little bodywork. But after she arrived, she rifled around looking for something that she said was hers. She seemed pretty upset about it. I gave her a little work. Later, I got a massage out of her. It wasn't half-bad. I really needed it."

"And you would like for me to believe this story?"

"What do you mean?"

"Given everything else that's already gone down? You set this one up on purpose. Maybe not consciously, but it's a sure bet you said something casually like, 'I'll be in Marin. Come on by if you are in the 'hood.' Did you say that?"

"But you didn't want to get together with me."

"That is so not the point. No one just pops by happening to be in the neighborhood from fucking Castro Valley. You are flirting with her."

Shaman walks into the dressing room and throws the sheets on the floor. As he reaches up to get a fresh set, he says, "She likes to flirt."

"Are you fucking kidding me? That really hurts my feelings."

He brings back a set of fresh flannel sheets and sets them on the table. "I'm sorry. That was uncalled for. I'm really tired. I am also having a hard time with the limitations on us. I really wanted to be with you last night. The situation frustrates me."

He makes up the table and says, "I'm gonna put another log on the fire. Lemme make it up to you. Why don't you lie down and let me give you a little work on your neck?"

When I reach up to feel it, my neck aches. It feels blocked on the right side. I lie down, fully dressed. I don't want to send mixed messages, but I'm also craving for him to show he cares for me.

We say nothing as he begins to work on my neck. Even if I decide I no longer want to be his lover, his having a piece of ass on the side is a foregone conclusion. Like handing off a baton or something. It is obvious that I am having a hard time letting go. But I've also got a kid. I can't administer to him night and day. Nor should I have to.

"That woman is out of control."

"I can see that now."

"And you are fanning the flames of a cat fight?"

"Let me focus on what I'm doing for a moment, will you?" He manipulates my neck first left then right then left again. He finishes by adjusting it with a loud crack.

As my neck unwinds, I choose to view this experience as the tremendous compliment that it actually is. I have the opportunity to be in competition with a beautiful woman who is several years my junior, all for the extraordinary luxury of picking up this man's sexual slack. I can either laugh my ass off at the absurdity of this situation, or I can chew on every last bone.

I like gristle. Here I am on the table again continuing to procrastinate in blatant disregard of the colonic currently being administered to me by the universe. Steadfast, I cling to my judgments about Ernesto and his growing relationship with Star. It is precisely this judgment that is making me fearful that I am not special to him at all.

Specialness, of course, is not exclusive to me. All sentient beings on the planet are special. But I am still too busy grounding myself externally to notice this truth. In fact, I'm just about to tell Ernesto what he needs to do for me so I can feel better about myself (and it is a very long list at this point), when he looks down at me, suddenly clairvoyant.

Like a shout-out from the universe he says, "You are vibrating at a different frequency, and more quickly, than I am. We're not in resonance. You'll get tired of all this."

He looks around the studio and gives a specific nod to the liquor cabinet. "The women, the booze, the drugs, the partying."

He concludes with a definitive, "You will leave this place." The power of Ernesto's proclamation stops me short. I am mute. I don't want to leave this place. I love this studio, *our* studio.

As if in response to my internal monologue, my right index finger begins to itch. "My right index finger is itching," I say.

Ernesto takes hold of my finger and begins to massage it as he explains, "This finger is the beginning of the large intestine meridian pathway. In yogic terms, it is also called the Jupiter finger and is related to expansion."

Innately, it would seem that my body knows that I need to grow. Ernesto is right. Can I let him be right just this once?

I sink deeper into the table and try to distract myself from an oncoming sense of panic. The thought of expanding professionally without him is overwhelming, so I willfully change the subject. "What's in the white bag?" I ask.

I point to a bag sitting on the kitchen counter. Shaman looks visibly relieved not to be going any further down our former verbal pathway. "It's for you."

"When are you going to give it to me?"

He reaches over to the kitchen counter and says, "First things first."

He picks up a slip of yellow paper and hands it to me.

I look at it. It is a gift certificate for a Vedic astrology reading. "That one is from me," he says.

Then he picks up the white bag and hands it to me and says, "This one is from Jean."

There is something in the way he hands it to me—maybe it is simply the firelight catching on the whiteness of the bag—that causes me to remember the dream I had about Jean. In the dream, she handed me a white bag that is shaped exactly like her bag.

As I make this connection, I know, like a flicker out in my peripheral vision, that something is off about the gift. I can't intellectually grasp what it is, but on a gut level, it spooks me. Immediately, I feel the same dread that held me as I awoke from that dream.

I have no idea why. So I dismiss it. Inside the bag is a case filled with small bottles of essential oils. There is also a note from Jean written on a piece of paper. Her loopy handwriting instructs, "Meditate on each plant. Your meditation will give you a deeper understanding of the oils themselves."

I've been learning to use various essential oils in my work and have wanted to further my understanding. Recently I emailed Jean to see if she might recommend a class for me locally but—come to think of it!—I never did hear back. But now it is clear. This present is her response.

I am touched by her thoughtfulness and oddly excited to have this gift from her. I get up off the table. I kiss Shaman's cheek. Bag in hand, I walk over to the kitchen counter. I pause for a moment to look out the windows and appreciate the winter chill settling over the afternoon. I look back at him. "I've decided it's time to write my memoir. I'm thinking of calling it *Disciple's Dilemma*. What do you think?"

"Catchy title." He rakes his eyes over me. That same old lust fills the space between us.

"I've got to go pick up India." I head back down the path feeling like this new medicine bag is somehow my graduation present.

JEAN

It's not easy being on the receiving end of this kind of love. I cross the bridge, clear that Ernesto is overdoing it. He seems to be a victim of what he himself calls self-sabotage. But I'm trying not to label his behavior last night as negative. Maybe this all sounds like a big excuse, but sometimes it is just part of the territory of knowing someone. Either that or I am being completely codependent. I mean, I was raised by my father. I oughta know.

I think back to my childhood bedroom—the one that is now India's—next to the kitchen. Historically, the liquor cabinet was located next to the kitchen doorway where the bottles nestled amidst the pots and pans. This meant that every time I went into the kitchen, I passed my dad's fire water.

Come to think of it, just like I do every day when I walk into the studio where Ernesto's bottles of hooch reside in a cabinet on a big frying pan. I don't know why I haven't ever figured out the echo and symmetry of this until now.

As a child, I used to sit in the doorway to the kitchen and watch my father chug Smirnoff straight out of a half-gallon bottle. He called this a rammer. On the backside of his swig, he'd smack his lips and say, "Smooth," drawing out the vowels. Then he'd say, "I drive better drunk than sober." This was right before he put me in the car to drive me somewhere.

Our tacit agreement was that I wouldn't say anything. I don't know how we got to this agreement, but by the time I was in middle school, we certainly had. The whole transaction was pretty much about him being a bad boy, and my job was to babysit us both and appreciate his naughtiness. And I've so been there ever since. The second time was in my one and only marriage, but then I was still really young. I graduated my senior year, pregnant and married to a loser stoner.

But now, for better or worse, I'm a grown woman. I know better. I also know that the anxiety Ernesto's behavior provokes in me is as much about my childhood or young adulthood as it is about anything else. If anything, our relationship is teaching me how to stop running defense. Ernesto's body and how he chooses to live in it is his business.

As I wait for the light to change on Lombard, I keep reminding myself to find the places in me that feel stuck rather than overly focus on Ernesto and what he is or isn't doing. I also haven't forgotten his proclamation that I will "leave this place." I know it's pretty unrealistic to imagine that there will be less drama despite our latest conversation.

But magical thinking is just that. As the light turns green, my thoughts drift to Ernesto's present. His gift is my ticket out of this conundrum. The stars shall alleviate my dilemma. It is time for me to use my gift certificate with the Vedic astrologer.

The very next morning, I call to make an appointment for my reading. The astrologer, a woman named Ty Coulter, picks up. She says she has time later that afternoon. I book it and drive over to Larkspur in the rain. She greets me at the gate wearing an Indian tunic. It glows hot pink in the gray light against her dark skin. She is barefoot, with a golden toe ring, and her black hair is long and thick.

She is younger than I expected. She leads me into her kitchen. We sit down at the table, and she reviews my alignments.

After a few minutes, she looks up at me and says, "You have an amazing chart, Vera." I am surprised. "Really. You do. You have the capacity to be famous. Do you know how Vedic astrology works? Vedic astrology works from an astrological vantage point that is some thirty degrees different from the Western one."

From the Vedic perspective, things are good. I wish I felt that way. I make a brief request for guidance in regard to my work environment. She zeroes in and says, "You got your training wheels in that studio. Now it's time for you to work at a different level. All the information you need is already inside you."

I feel like asking, "What? Do you have a crystal ball or something?" I abstain from being a smartass.

After a minute or two more of looking over my karmic coordinates, she says, "Take everything out of your field that does not ground you. Your work is your medicine."

"How much medicine do I have to take?" I ask. So much for abstinence.

She tilts her head at me. "What?"

"What I meant to say, is staying in the studio productive?"

"Close your eyes and meditate on what staying feels like."

I close my eyes. When I focus on the sensation of staying, my gut feels like it is host to a backhoe. In fact, my entire midriff seems to be undergoing deconstruction at the mere notion. Instead, I say, "I have butterflies in my stomach."

Her response is only seven words long. "*Get this man out of your way.*"

She goes on to talk about various transits that I can't remember. I thank her, walk outside, and sit in my car in the rain. I look at my cell. By now, I am sensible enough to know that sharing this reading is absolutely not in my best interest, but I also told Ernesto I'd call him when the reading was over.

He sounds sleepy. Yawning into the phone, he says, "You woke me up." This is really unusual for him. He never takes naps. "I'm still here," he says. "I had an impromptu client, but she canceled. I'm curled up in our bed with a fire. My afternoon is free, baby. Wanna come over and cuddle?"

"Aw, that is so sweet, but I can't," I say pleading motherhood. "I need to pick up India." This isn't technically true for a couple hours, but I somehow can't bring myself to reject his invitation outright.

He says, "My client base is dropping off. It isn't something that I like to talk about."

I think to myself, *I'm not getting a lot of interest in my work either.* "Oh, well. Don't overthink it. Sometimes it's a little slow," I say before we hang up.

I sign off feeling worn out and tired and like all I really want to do is go over there and cuddle with him. I sit there considering that not listening to my common sense is, indeed, an option. I mean I've done it before—more than once!—and still lived to tell the tale. Despite the bad behavior, I also have to admit that I am still into him, which—I well know—is either the biggest part of my problem or makes me pathetic.

The stars, however, have just told me to leave him and to leave the T Room. Just in case I've forgotten, I am still sitting in Ty, the Vedic astrologer's, driveway where I am having issues with the ephemeral nature of my short-term memory, a part of my thinking brain that seems to emanate from between my legs.

I acknowledge that restraint is not all it's cracked up to be, not even close, as I point my car back in the direction of the city. When I pull up in front of our house, my cell dings with a message from Jean. She says she's coming down tomorrow, Thursday Friday evening, for a reading with the Vedic astrologer. She wants to know if she can use the studio Friday night and adds that she is "wide-open" to get together with me. The good news is she sounds friendly. The bad news is Ernesto gave us the same present.

I say she can use the place. And as far as her offer for a get-to-gether goes, I think, *Oh, what the hell?* Creating a more above-board friendship with her seems like a good way to start separating myself romantically from Ernesto. I say yes. We set a coffee date for early the following Saturday morning before my first client.

When the morning day of our rendezvous arrives, I leave India in bed in the city curled up with Francisco. Then I head to the studio to meet Jean.

It's raining, so I'm wearing my jacket and slouchy old felt hat adorned with the silver Navajo pin of a scorpion that has a chunk of turquoise on its back tail. I negotiate my way up the slick pathway. Gently knocking on the door, I wait to enter until I hear Jean say, "Come in."

As I step over the threshold, the place feels like ice. Whenever she is in town, the fireplace stands unused, and the empty yawn, especially on a day like today, seems peculiar.

But it is more than that. All the lamps in the studio, the ones that give the place its warm and cozy glow, are off. This would not seem so strange except that the only light turned on is the worst one in the joint. Located above the table, this overhead light feels cold and clinical; neither Ernesto nor I ever use it. But, located on the massage chair next to the table, sits Jean directly underneath the light, illuminated by its eerie glare.

There is an efficient intensity about her. It's almost as if I've interrupted her doing something. The table, however, is empty; only her purse sits beside her. Her bag is packed, standing sentry by the door.

The whole place feels off. I turn a full 360 degrees to my left, as the recurring itch on the right side of my nose, located along what Shaman calls my stomach meridian line, rings like an alarm bell. Unconsciously, I scratch away.

I pull up a zafu while Jean moves to the chair across from me.

This is where my clients always sit. So why do I suddenly feel like I'm working?

"Thank you for giving me the essential oil kit," I say trying to set a positive tone between us. "That was so sweet of you."

Instead of replying, Jean asks, "Did my husband give you a gift too?"

My stomach clenches. I know what she is talking about. The gift certificate for the Vedic astrology reading. Giving us both the same present is not only bad marital politics, but straight-up stupid. Ernesto leveled the playing field with this maneuver. The fact that Jean has to share her present with me was not nice of him.

But it is also not my fault. Today, for once, I have nothing to hide. I take a deep inhale into my gut in order to clear the sensation that I am somehow wrong or bad, and say, "Yes, he did."

There it is, my honesty, just sitting in the mush pot between us, giving us both the opportunity to take a good look at it.

"Did you like the Vedic astrologer?"

I say, "Yes." Being honest feels healthy.

With an odd look, Jean tells me, "Ty says *I* am the mother."

I almost fall off my zafu. I cannot create a better description for Jean. Of course, she is, she's the mother. She deserves quantum kudos for being an uber-mommy. And mostly to him. "I agree."

I notice that she doesn't bother to ask me what the Vedic astrologer said about me and choose to be grateful as we pull our coats on. We decide to head into Tam Junction for coffee. Ernesto regularly complains that Jean is a terrible passenger, so I let her take the wheel of her Subaru.

As she drives us, I mention the knot I have firmly lodged in the back of my scapula, on the left side of my heart. Her eyes appraise me. I've never noticed before, but there is something otherworldly about the pale gray of her irises.

Her knuckles whiten as she clutches the wheel tighter. Then she says, "When we get back, I'll show you an exercise to help strengthen and stretch that area." Seems simple enough.

After we finish, I excuse myself to go to the bathroom. When I return, her anxiety is so palpable that—like a bad contact high—I start feeling anxious too, and wonder what can possibly be making her so tense.

As we pull back in front of the studio, she seems even more wound up. Mystified, I follow her back up the path. As she walks into the cottage, her back turned to me, she murmurs something like, "Why don't you take some time off?"

Her left hand grazes the top of the massage table as she turns back toward me, smiling. Her suggestion is so far out in left field. The right side of my nose begins to itch again. Annoyed, I take an absentminded swipe at it as I head for the laundry room, where I've left that clutch of turkey feathers.

Ernesto called me the day before, requesting some feathers for the spear that he is now making for himself. As an offering, I decide to give a couple of feathers to both Ernesto and Jean. I guess you can call these feathers my version of a peace offering.

When I return, I can't help noticing that same strange smile tacked onto Jean's face. She asks, "Are these the feathers you found on your pilgrimage?"

Again, there is something about her question that strikes me as strange. But I don't dwell on it. I sit down on the table while she selects two feathers. Then I ask, "Do you have feathers at home?"

She smiles again shaking her head from side to side.

This is bullshit. I happen to know that there are some very nice feathers sitting in the massage room. But again, swept up in the spirit of being collegial, I dismiss her lie and offer two more feathers.

She sits quietly stroking them before pulling another one out for Ernesto. "This is for Ernesto." Next, she chooses a beat-up, black crow feather, saying, "And this one's for me."

It is the most bedraggled feather of the bunch. I actually found it on the porch of the cottage around the same time I had that dream about her handing me the key.

As promised, she offers to help me work on my neck. "Why don't you lie down over there in front of the mirror, Vera." She pulls a bolster out from under the bed.

I lie on the bolster, face up, arms out, crucifixion style. I continue to think about what an odd choice the black crow feather is. Then out of nowhere, she looks down at me and says it again: "You've been working so hard, Vera. Why don't you consider taking some time off?"

My body jumps and twitches a little in response. This is the second time this morning she's made the suggestion. Come to think of it, this is something she has said every so often over the last few months. But until now, I never really paid much attention to it. Most of the time, I've been too preoccupied with my sense of purpose. But now I have to wonder, *Why is she repeating herself?*

I may not know why on a conscious level, but on an instinctual level, it makes me extremely uneasy. Here I am, once again on the receiving end of work being done by a practitioner with whom I do not feel entirely comfortable. In fact, when I catch our reflection in the big floor-to-ceiling mirror that stands behind us, I can't help but notice that her posture has a disturbing predatory quality to it. As she manipulates my neck, my body feels both young and entirely defenseless.

The exercise, however, seems simple enough, so I thank her. As I get up, I feel a little dizzy.

I say, "I'll be right back. I need to pee."

When I return, the front door is wide open, and she is standing on the porch, off to the left, holding her bags, giving off an urgent vibe, like it's all she can do to not bolt. As she begins a brisk walk down the pathway, I grab my hat to follow her. Something about the hat looks wrong, but Jean is on a mission, and I don't have time to think about it. I chase after her feeling like a puppy nipping at her heels, wondering why I care if this woman likes me or is pleased with me.

As she sweeps out onto the street, I call out to her back, thanking her for our date. I go on to say, "I'm so grateful for everything I've learned in these last months," and conclude with, "I have never had a stronger sense of self."

She stops, turns back toward me, and stares. Her face looks wizened. She mutters something incomprehensible. Then she gets into her car and drives off without saying good-bye. The taillights on the back of her freshly detailed Subaru illuminate red. I am left standing in her dust, feeling unsure. I have just given her an enormous compliment, so why did she look stricken?

I turn my gaze down to the hat in my hands—it's then I notice that my scorpion pin is gone.

VERA

The scorpion pin cannot have fallen off my hat—its catch is broken closed, and it takes a lot of focus to get it to release. Also the fabric of my hat is torn in the place where the pin has always been.

I try to remember if I snagged it on anything. Bummed, I walk back through the gate. As I walk up the pathway, I scan the bushes on either side. I look around the front porch. Nada. After exhausting all my ideas for where it might be, I go into the studio, build a fire, light a candle next to White Tara, and mute the harsh florescent lighting. This day, I think, is off to a troubling start.

A few hours later I finish work, feeling like crap. This is not something new. I often feel nauseated while I work. But increasingly, I feel sick even when I'm not working. This has begun to concern me. I feel toxic somehow, as if this life I am living is poisoned.

I've already had a physical and gotten my blood work done. In both cases, I'm good. The official Western medical model deems me basically healthy. Nevertheless, I am—day by day—feeling progressively worse. I begin to wonder if it is actually possible to lift physical symptoms off the people you're in contact with, as happens with both emotional and energetic vibes.

I currently have a client with severe yeast infections. As I think about it, I realize that every single time I work with her, I feel slightly self-disgusted afterward, as if I am somehow ingesting whatever's ailing her. Ernesto has never said that this could be a part of what I think of as the healing transaction. I don't think it has ever crossed his mind. Even entertaining it on my end is a stretch. But, as I begin to question this idea, could this also mean that I can be physically affected by other people's use of drugs or alcohol?

This is a wild concept. But, seriously, given the extent of my symptoms today, I feel like I don't want to trade work with Ernesto anymore. For that matter, I don't want to work with a few of my clients either.

I need to talk to someone other than Ernesto about this. As she is the closest thing I've ever had to a therapist, I decide to go see my regular astrologer. I trust her and know she can hang with questions that seem pretty out there to me. Plus, my father is the one who sent me to her in the first place.

As it turns out, Annie can see me late the following Monday afternoon up in Fairfax. It has been a while since our last reading, and it feels good to be sitting on her corduroy sofa once again. I like this older woman whose silver hair is tucked into a messy bun. As requested, she looks over Ernesto's chart in conjunction with my own. Then she asks, "Are you getting into a power struggle with Ernesto and his wife?"

I say, "No . . . I mean, maybe . . . I mean, why?"

"Because it shows up right here." She points to a series of triangles, squares, and lines, calling them alignments. To me, they look more like obstructions in my house of something. I may be consistently blown away by its accuracy, but I have yet to understand the complex symbol system of astrology.

"I know. I'm trying to accept the limitations of my dynamic with him. I'm attempting to be just friends. I'm trying to do the same with Jean."

When Annie raises her eyebrows, I say, "I know. Right. Total crazy town. Literally, I'm thinking of inviting a bunch of colleagues over for pizza and including them."

Annie looks happy. "Good work on a karmic level. I've been wondering what's going to happen. See this?"

My eyes follow the length of her extended index finger, which is encircled by a beautiful gold-and-amethyst ring. She points to what, at least from my perspective, looks like a multi colored gridlock in my chart. She says, "There is a place here, between the two of you, where it looks as if you might be together in the long run. But you remember what I've always told you, don't you? This man is not monogamous—this is written all over his chart. But here's this, Vera. You are!"

I look down at our collective astrology. On a basic temperamental level, he and I are coming from two different planets. As the old book says, he is from Mars, and I am from Venus.

I've known this about our stars from early on, but I was too busy fucking him. And this is the first time Annie has ever said that I might choose to be with him anyway. What this would look like is not all that hard to imagine. I'm already on this ride. Stolen meetings and midnight trysts with other women. I stare glumly down at our astrological bottleneck.

I chew on my next question. "Is it possible for me to actually lift physical symptoms off people?"

Annie looks shocked. "Absolutely—don't you know this about yourself?"

"No. Of course I don't."

"Didn't he teach you how to clean your body?"

"No. He didn't teach me anything about cleaning anything."

"What the hell is he doing out there?"

A thousand possibilities come to mind, "Hmmm?" I say, "Sex? Drugs? Alcohol?"

"You have to clean your body every day. You do not have to reinvent the wheel. There are ancient yogic systems in place for exactly this purpose. It is essential that you do this."

I sink more deeply into the corduroy, not wanting to hear this, even though it is a wisdom that I already intrinsically know. My body is intricately related to everyone else I am in contact with, whether I happen to like it or not.

"Does this mean I am affected by the booze and drugs and all his promiscuity?"

"Of course, you are, Vera. How could you not be?"

This is not good news. Especially if I want to continue to share a studio with him. "But I have feelings for him," I say as the tears begin to splash down across our mutual transit.

"I know, Vera. Trust me. Your attraction for one another is all over both of your charts. But you have really gotten the best of him already—it's all downhill from here. There is substance abuse stuff right here. Look." She points again. "Do you see this?"

"What does it mean?"

"He has an insatiable desire to consume just about everything. I don't want one of those things to be you."

Ugh. Still I ask, "Can I stay in our workspace?"

She looks down at our collective astrology for a long time. With the patience of an elder talking to the small child in me, she smiles through her glasses. "Vera, he cannot let you shine beside him. Your capacity for faithfulness and loyalty is truly a beautiful quality. But in this case, it is not your friend. Your faithfulness is, in fact, holding you back."

The stars do not lie. Regardless of how many degrees of separation there are from this astrological vantage point and the Vedic one, they share the same truth. I have now heard it twice. I ask, "So now what?"

"There is a man coming in for you, Vera. Open yourself up so you can meet him."

Her little dog jumps up onto the sofa and starts snuggling me. Annie looks up and says, "You might like that, wouldn't you?"

My small voice says, "Yes."

"OK, then! Get out of that place. It will be good for your intimacy."

"Are you sure?"

"I know it will be."

The next morning, Tuesday, I wake up with an astrological hangover. I've overslept, and my head is pounding. I can hear India thumping on our collective wall. She yells, "Mom, you up?"

I pick up my phone. It reads 7:55 a.m. Shit, I'm already really late. I jump out of the sack to take a cursory glance at my haggard reflection in the mirror over the dresser. There is a huge zit to the right side of my nose. Like a bull's-eye, it is located exactly where I have that recurring itch. Given the urgency of our departure, I have no choice but to leave this volcano intact.

I get into the car, wearing something resembling my pajamas. Already waiting in the passenger seat with Francisco on her lap, India orders, "Go. I've got a chem exam at eight fifteen."

I pull a U-turn out of Pompeii, onto Polk, and head west down Greenwich Street to Van Ness. India heaves an audible sigh of frustration. Clearly, I am not driving fast enough.

Just then, our vehicle screeches like a dying cat. I stamp down on the accelerator and try to make it through the yellow light on Van Ness. Right in the middle of the intersection, the car stalls out. As the light turns red, I watch oncoming traffic accelerate toward us. We slide backwards toward the northbound curb and manage to coast downhill. When we near Lombard, I am able to restart the engine, but just as quickly, the car dies. This leaves me no choice but to stagnate in the crosswalk, sweating.

India begins to have a total meltdown. "Here," I say shoving a credit card and cash at her for her lunch, saying, "Get an Uber!"

"But it's surge, Mom. It's too expensive."

"Go," I say, "Surge? Fuck surge. I don't give a shit!"

After I watch her get into one an Uber, I call AAA. Soon after, I am rescued by a total hottie who simply tows my car to the mechanic instead of asking me out on a date.

As Frank and I walk back up the hill, I keep my eyes down, hoping not to run into anyone I know. I eat toast, drink the coffee I never had, and take an overdue shower. As I emerge, my phone rings with a call from my technician. His diagnosis is that my car's harmonic balancer is shot. I don't even know what a harmonic balancer is, but my vehicle is not going anywhere without a new one. Naturally, this, along with the new set of tires I've been needing, will cost close to four grand. FML.

Later that evening, Ernesto and Jean call me together on speakerphone. Normally, a joint call would have been icky, but given the conditions of our new era, it feels almost a little like family. Evidently, they are having an evening cocktail and say they simply want to check in.

Ernesto brings me up to date up-to-date on some details regarding the studio, while Jean listens in the background. Almost as if charmed by the whole familial transaction, I decide to tell them the story about my car. I say, "I am interpreting this new development as an automotive metaphor for the condition of my body. My own harmonic balance feels shot."

Immediately, Jean says, "Why don't you use the new kit I gave you, Vera? It will help you support your immune system."

After dinner, I get the case and bring it into the kitchen. I set it down onto the table next to India and her computer.

There is a sheet from the company that makes this essential oil kit with directions explaining how to muscle test yourself for what your body intuitively needs. Step one is to take the thumb and pinky of your left hand and connect them while extending the three remaining fingers. I do.

Step two is to insert a bottle on the palm of your hand.

I select a bottle of lavender oil and—not very effectively—try to balance it on my palm. It clatters onto the table.

Step three is to see if the thumb and pinky remain strong with said oil or break apart.

I squeeze my thumb and pinky together so hard I fumble the bottle again. It hits the floor but doesn't break.

From his bed, Francisco perks up his ears as India looks up from her laptop. "Mom, what the bloody hell are you doing?"

"I am trying to teach myself how to muscle test my body to see if I need any of these essential oils for my immune system."

India rolls her eyes.

Picking up the bottle, I unscrew the stopper and liberally anoint my left hand. Putting both hands together and rubbing hard to create friction, I inhale deeply.

"Let me guess who gave you that?"

"Not him—this is a present from his wife, Jean."

"Oh, terrific, Mom. That doesn't make it any better. When are you going to dump those pervs? You don't think it's strange that now they're both calling you. Like for what? What are they doing? What do they want? A threesome? Or are they just fucking with you and your generosity? You are being way naïve!"

"No, I'm not. And I don't think it's weird. I think it's nice. Ernesto and I are coworkers. Why can't we all be friends?"

"Mom, because Jean hates your guts! If I were you, I would just get the hell out of there. The first step is to pitch that bag. There's something really creepy about it."

"Don't be so dramatic," I say. But in all honesty, as I continue to go through the process of teaching myself how to muscle test, I feel more muddled than I do clear. In fact, now I feel a lot less confident in my ability to take care of myself. Figuring I just need to take a class on essential oils, I go to bed.

I get up the following Wednesday morning with a small rash on my ring finger. I look at it, wondering if I could have picked up a case of poison oak. But I'm also armed with a new sense of resolve. I grab a Zipcar car, drop India off at school, the reluctant Francisco at daycare, and then Google "Yoga fast and easy ways to clean the body." I scroll down to discover a bunch of different practices to strengthen my aura.

My aura is the energetic field that I emanate and that surrounds me twenty-four/seven. My aura has no downtime. Nor does it ever get to go on vacation. However, I am open to almost anything at this point, so I get busy reading how to clean my aura.

This mostly entails doing repetitive movements from both seated and standing positions. While seated I blow air out of my mouth rapidly in a breath work technique called breath of fire. If I included a paper bag to huff and puff into, most people would call this heavy breathing a form of hyperventilating. While I do so sans the bag, my arms are extended up over my head palms forward. Once I finish the cycle of breath work, I am directed to connect my hands via the tips of my thumbs. If I can do so effortlessly, it is apparently a show of my connectedness to the great beyond. When I try, my palms pass each other like freighters in the night, my thumbs completely miss.

Next, I stand up and bend over with my hands on the floor and lift my right leg behind me. I pump my body up and down multiple times, like a version of standing push-ups before I switch legs. After that I sit down on the floor again and extend my arms out in front of me. I interlace my hands with the inside of my wrists touching and pump my arms up and down for two to three minutes. Lastly, I open my arms out on either side of me at a forty-five-degree angle, palms facing front, and close and open in rapid sequence until the *ping* of a text distracts me.

Instantly conscripted, I abandon my new practice to discover a text from the sexy masseur from Esalen. Totally out of the blue, this is the first time Will Carver has been in touch since our collision on the massage table. My aura must be very shiny indeed.

HEY VERA COMING TO THE BAY TOMORROW FREE TO TRADE?

I decide I can look at this potential sexual development from two perspectives. Either I'm an asshole and behaving just like Ernesto, or I'm creating a new venue.

LOVE TO COME TO MY STUDIO?

No sooner do I seal the deal than Ernesto texts, saying that he has to come down to the Bay too. He will be arriving tomorrow, Thursday, and needs to spend the night. I only have one client on Thursday. This is totally ridiculous from a money perspective.

I text Will and ask, CAN WE MEET EARLIER AND CHANGE THE VENUE? Blessedly, he's flexible, so I reroute him to our house during school hours. Thursday morning, Will is on his way to my house for our trade when India walks into my bedroom complaining, "Mom, I feel sick."

I put my hand on her forehead. She feels fine. Incapable of removing the obvious touch of exasperation in my voice, I say, "Honey, you don't feel warm."

"I want to stay home from school."

"No possible way." My voice has the hard-assed maternal agenda of a woman trying very hard to get laid by someone other than the man that she co-rents her studio with.

"But why?"

"Because it is not gonna happen is why." Softening a bit, I add, "I have a work appointment at the house."

This is technically true, for my current work seems to involve releasing my selfhood via my vagina. I shut the door on any further possibility of negotiation.

All the way to school, I endure India's grumbling about how I am so mean! When she opens her door, I have to restrain myself from pushing her out at the curb. Francisco reclaims shotgun, as I blast back down California Street, in quest of my salvation.

A short while thereafter, I open the front door. Will walks in looking hot. Organic and free trade, he lifts me up as I wrap my legs around his waist. He carries me straight down the hall and into my kitchen and takes me right then and there on the hardwood table with a dishrag under my butt.

In bed a little later, I tell Will, "It feels like a hundred years since I've had a man in my own bed."

He grabs my ass and says, "And to think you don't look a day over ninety-nine."

This makes me want to invite him back. However, the next time he comes into town, on a Monday, I have the exact same experience. Ernesto has some sort of emergency. India tries to stay home from school. And my handyman, who is named—I am so not kidding—Shorty Butts wants to come fix my sticky front door.

Against all karmic odds, I am still determined to get laid. Sans shower, valiantly, I open my front door to the sound of Will's knock. He cruises in. Right out of the gate, he picks me up again, biceps popping, but this time he lifts me right on up over his head as he carries me into the kitchen. I laugh outrageously as he whirls me around.

"Stop! The g-forces are setting in."

"I certainly hope so."

Snicker, snicker. It's a real pep squad maneuver. Not that I have ever been on one. But I am sure willing to try. There is something about those pom-poms. Naturally I am already concocting the outfit as he lowers me against his buffed chest. I wrap my legs around his waist when my dark Adonis whispers in my ear, "Let's go wrestle, baby girl."

Bingo. He carries me down the hall to my bed for a second time. After he lays me down, he strips me before flipping me over to pull my flimsy thong aside. Then without further ado, he takes me from behind. What's not to like?

Sex with this guy is like being pinned by a boulder. Will is a big man who has—true to cultural stereotype—a huge cock. This, unto itself, is no small measure and feels like liberation. I am not challenged in all the ways that I have formerly deemed to be significant, the niceties, such as dinner first? But I am met by his density. And he is generous and attentive in the sack.

Things are on the upswing, until he flips me back over and sticks his head between my legs. He takes a harder than necessary nip on my clit and says, "I am going to make you scream."

As if on cue, even though I already texted that this morning is out, Shorty's skill saw whines from the front door. It's so loud, he actually sounds like he is in my house. I throw on a robe and open the door to look down the hallway and, sure enough, my front door is fucking open. Furthermore, is screaming a prerequisite to the orgasm that, at this point, it does not look like I am going to get? I object.

It is simply inconceivable that it should be this hard for a consenting adult to get laid in the privacy of her own bed. Twice.

STAR

Later that same day, Monday, dressing for work, I feel like I am walking through sludge. The studio looks old, tired, and in need a fresh paint job. Two out of my three clients cancel. I seem to spend more time cranking up the mat, shoving in a pair of earplugs, and having a snooze than I do working.

I've just finished dragging myself off the table, when I see that I have a phone message from Ernesto on my cell. I decide to return his call on the home line, thinking, "Should be no prob—we've got nothing to hide."

When Jean answers the phone, I say, "Hi, it's Vera; I'm simply returning Ernesto's call."

She explains, "*We* are busy working on something that *we* are working on, but you can call *us* back later because *we* are home." She wraps up with, "Love you!" and disconnects.

Then it dawns on me. They are having a class on their property this weekend, and Ernesto has asked me if I want to assist in teaching. This is to be my coming-out party. It's the first time that any of their students has been invited to do this. Ernesto has already told me that it's cool with Jean, but after listening to her on this phone call, while her response may be "yes" to him, it is a definite "no" to me.

This is the kind of stuff we study. How mixed messages affect the body. The Sherlock in me deduces, *Jean is so not acknowledging her feelings*. I feel a sudden lust for a good houndstooth cape and magnifying glass in order to deduce why. But I also have no desire to talk to "*them*" on the phone either. So I blow off calling them back and do a lot of thinking about my call with Jean instead. It's the indirect nature of it that's disconcerting. But in the end, it's not like a light bulb goes off or anything. All I really feel is pooped out from trying to vivisect her behavior.

When Ernesto arrives in town for work on Tuesday, he tells me he is coming into the city afterward to have a drink with Grace. I decide to invite him over for an impromptu dinner in honor of our evolving friendship. I mean, why not?

When I go to answer the front door, he is winding up a phone call looking completely worn out. As he walks in, his first words to me are, "She says 'hello.'" He then elaborates. "She is spending the evening alone."

I think he is talking about Grace, but then I realize that by "she," Ernesto, of course, means Jean. And come to think of it, "she" is always spending the evening alone. Recently, he has been in Tam Junction more often than usual. I wonder how she feels about that. But I let the question go as I move aside for Ernesto to walk in the door.

We commend ourselves on our ability to be friends. We even do a little victory dance around the redwood table where I so recently acquired splinters in my derriere.

He laughs, but when I stop to lean over to pull some store-bought lasagna out of the oven, I catch that same look in his eyes.

We have just finished eating when India walks in from a meeting. India is on a task force wherein she and her fellow students, as volunteers, plant trees anywhere people will let them.

She says, "My back is killing me."

"Lie down on the floor," says Ernesto.

I'm shocked yet pleased when she says, "OK."

That she's actually open to Ernesto getting down on the floor and doing a little work with her is remarkable. Francisco springs up from his dog bed to cover her face in smooches. This is when the whole thing between us finally becomes easy. It's almost as if it has always been like this, as if we are an extended family that I crave for us to be. Then we all lie around, hanging out talking on our daybed, until India and Francisco leave for her room.

After her departure, Ernesto sits up with dark circles under his eyes. I wonder if I look as trashed as he does. As my bedroom is off limits to all things Ernesto, I suggest that he stay put on the daybed.

Almost immediately, he begins to snore. I listen to him as I clean up. When I'm done, I try to wake him, but for all practical purposes, he is out, unconscious. I pull off his clothes and go get my duvet. I put it over him. I go change into a T-shirt and leggings and return to climb in next to him. I fit my body into his, relieved not to be making love with him. Later, in the dark he slips out, dresses, and leaves.

He calls me later that Wednesday night in tears to say that his had been the only car on the bridge. According to him, "Crossing the bridge felt like some kind of mother portal."

His snoring the night before had been so damn loud that all I feel in response is tired. Mother portal? Fuck that, Mr. E.

"Thanks for the dinner. India is so amazing. The lasagna was delicious. You are a class act, baby. I am totally into you, Vera." Then he slurs something about needing to go get a bite to eat.

I hang up feeling like hell. Is he now turning into a total lush or what?

After he leaves town early Thursday, I head over to the studio for work. When my last client leaves, I discover a note from Ernesto. He has made it for me from a *New Yorker* cartoon. It is titled "OMG." Underneath the cartoon, he has written, "I love everything about us."

I'm about to call him to tell him how sweet he is when I hear foot-steps on the front porch outside. I turn my head just in time to see a woman's body through the window as the door opens to reveal Star in that same damn sweatshirt.

I need this woman in my space right now like I need a backhoe excavating my third eye. Then she has the gall to ask me in her inim-itable Star-like style, "What are you doing here?"

Where does she get off?

I put my hands on my hips and stand taller. I spread my feet hip width apart splaying my toes for maximum ballast. "If you haven't noticed, this is *my* studio space. I pay rent here." I maintain the pose. Everything about my posture says, *You just go ahead and fucking try me, girlfriend.* I do, however, have a worthy adversary. Instead of turning and skedaddling her butt back down *my* pathway, she comes on in and closes the door behind her. She stares me down.

I stare back. Hard. "What do you want, Star?"

"I'm dropping something off for Ernesto, so he'll have it when he comes back into town next week." She shifts her backpack off her shoulder like, *Here, see?*

I do. There is a slim brown paper bag sticking out of the open zipper. Of course, a bottle. This is rich.

I cross my arms across my chest. "First of all, what I do or don't do in regard to this studio is my business. And secondly, you are wel-come to give whatever that is to me or leave it there for him on the kitchen counter."

Star swings her backpack onto the kitchen counter. She pulls her sweatshirt off to reveal a neon jog bra two sizes too small. She pulls a family-sized bottle of gin out of the paper bag. She grasps the neck in her right fist like a barbell. "This gin is artisanal. I found it on sale at Costco for Ernesto. Are you serious?"

I look at the bottle. *Oh honey.* But before the endearment can cross my lips Star yells, "What in the hell makes you think I would let you give this to him? Are you fucking high? Look at what you did the last time I was here? You took something that was special to me, and you threw it away."

For a split second, I don't know what she's talking about. Then bingo. Right. The White Claw twelve-pack I poured down the drain, the bloody cans I recycled?

I volley, "Who calls White Claw *special*?" And that is all it takes for Star to launch herself at me wielding Ernesto's craft gin like a tennis racket.

Thank god the table is standing in her way, but just. She kickboxes it and catches her ankle around one of the legs. As the table shudders forward, she loses her balance. To save herself from a potential face plant, she releases the bottle. In slow motion, we both watch the bottle fly toward the stone where it crash-lands onto the edge of the hearth and shatters. The alcoholic botanical aroma of wild-gathered juniper berries is released as the clear liquid pools onto the studio floor.

I look up to my right just in time to catch White Tara winking at me. The goddess in the room thinks this is funny, as Star clearly does not. "No! Now look what you made me do!" She flings the table aside Kali-like and heads toward me, all rage and teeth.

I try to sidestep the aromatic puddle, wishing I had a cosmic toggle stick to bonk her with. You know, just to put us both out of our misery. But before I finish the fantasy I manage to slip on the liquid, and I end up in Holy Communion with the gin on the floor.

I weigh the debatable wisdom of leaning over to take a sip. I'm surrounded by broken glass and my sacrum, now bruised, is bathing in it. Thinking *I am so fucking pissed, man*, I lurch up onto my knees when, miraculously, she, too, loses her balance. Seeing her gluteus maximus hit the hardwood floor is satisfying to say the least.

Star scrabbles up on to her knees and takes a swipe at me, claws out, chipped fingernail polish. I slap her hand away a little harder than I intend to. She tries to catch herself and just barely avoids setting her hand down on a piece of broken glass.

"Holy shit! Star!"

She spits, "What do you want?"

"Look at that piece of glass next to your hand. You could have sliced it open. Take a deep breath and slow the fuck down."

"Excuse me? Where do you come from? Who are you to tell me what to do? You don't even fucking know!"

"Yes, I do. You just drove what? More than two hours to drop off a bottle for this asshole? This whole scenario is so not worth it. Trust me."

I take a couple of deep breaths to steady myself before adding, "I am so sorry."

Still defiant she pokes the air between us and asks, "Sorry about what?"

"I'm sorry about all of it." My eyes rake the broken bottle and the medicinal gin on the floor, and then it hits me. "But mostly I am sorry that I hurt your feelings. What I said wasn't nice. Nor was it necessary."

My apology takes her by surprise. She stops for a moment to rearrange herself. Her shoulders sag as the crackly atmosphere shifts to reveal our mutual vulnerability. The whole scenario feels just a little too close to home, so I make a half-assed attempt at humor. "I guess we just christened the joint, huh?"

Neither one of us laughs. It's not the T Room that's being christened. This is our 'take me to the river' moment. We are both taking a deep drink at the baptismal wellspring of female consciousness. Like why are we competing with each other over this guy, just for starters?

"Do you think he didn't care if I ran into you?"

Now I am the one who is surprised. I decide to pass on the lesson I recently learned at the Vedic astrologer. "Close your eyes. Take a moment. Ask yourself that question. What does your gut instinct tell you?"

Careful to avoid the glass, she moves around on the floor to readjust her legs into a cross-legged position. Silent, she closes her eyes. When she opens them, she looks off to the side as she swats a tear away from her left cheek. She looks back at me. The tip of her nose is red. "Son of a bitch."

I hold her gaze and nod. "Yeah. Believe me, I know." She remains sitting on the floor as I stand up and stretch. "I'm going to go get the mop. Want to help me clean this up?"

As I grab the mop from the closet and go back to the kitchen sink, I watch her on her hands and knees begin to collect pieces of the broken bottle. I turn on the faucet and squirt some Mrs. Meyers into the basin, as the water rises.

Out of nowhere I hear a small voice from behind me say, "Vera, will you mentor me?"

I'm stunned. I take my time putting the mop in the sink. "Star, I'm so flattered, but I don't even know—"

She cuts me off before I can finish, "Never mind. Just forget about it. It was a stupid idea anyway."

For a moment, she continues to shove the shattered glass into a pile. Suddenly she gets up off the floor and walks over to the kitchen counter looking frustrated. She ties her sweatshirt around her waist like she can't decide whether to hit me or hug me. Before she does either, she flings her backpack over her shoulder and stomps past me out the door.

I watch her stride back down the pathway as I finish my sentence out loud, "I don't even know how to take care of myself." I keep her in my line of sight until she turns the corner and is gone.

This performance has cured whatever ambivalence I may have had about leaving this place. I go sweep the pieces of the bottle into a dustpan and throw them in the trash under the kitchen sink. Next

I give the floor a good twice over. After that, I return to my original task.

23

pick up my cell and call him. When he answers, I say, "I need to talk with you about something important."

"I have some people here right now. I'll call you back tonight after Jean leaves for an overnight in the city."

A few hours later, I pick up my cell as it starts to chime. I finally say it. "I had another episode with Star. It is impossible to work here under these conditions."

"Why? What happened?"

"I don't even want to go into it. I'll talk to you about it when I see you at class tomorrow."

"Jesus! Are you alright? All I know is that she was in Costco and called me and—"

I interrupt him. "It doesn't matter. Remember when you told me that I was going to get tired of all this? Well I'm really tired right now."

I can hear him breathing on the other end. When he speaks, the timbre of his voice drops. I can hear him release the anxiety of waiting for me to do what we both know is inevitable.

He asks, "Will I still see you tomorrow?"

"Of course." I press END, scared shitless about how I am going to survive professionally. But I've been here before and know I'll figure it out. I just have to muscle my way through my exit, maintaining as much compassion as I can for both of us.

As Lady Luck would have it, India is working on a huge essay for English on *Fahrenheit 451* which, according to her, is the worst book ever written. Naturally, the essay is due the following Monday. She walks into my bedroom the next morning around seven.

"Mom, can I stay home from school?" she asks.

"Of course."

Now leaving is out of the question. India needs support in the form of encouragement and repeated trips to the grocery store. This means I have to do that thing that most single parents know how to do. It's called letting go.

I'm not willing to cancel the trip entirely though. As I am quite aware, no other student of Ernesto's has ever been invited to assist, and I am very inspired to do so. This is an opportunity not to miss. After I see the two clients I've got scheduled in the morning, I text Ernesto:

CAN'T GET OUT OF HERE TILL TOMORROW MORNING INDIA NEEDS ME AROUND FOR FOOD AND WATER

He responds: GET HERE WHEN YOU GET HERE TEX

I respond: OK

He texts: MISS YOU

I don't text him back that I miss him, even though it is true. When I get home and walk into the kitchen with a bag of groceries, I find India spread out across the kitchen table with an empty ice cream carton sitting next to her.

"I hate homework."

"That makes two of us. My next support group is called 'Mothers Against Homework.'"

India laughs. "That's my mom."

"Who came up with the idea that the average high school student has to be good at five to seven different subjects in the course of one day? No adult is ever asked to do this. Just look at that backpack." I point to her huge black backpack sitting on the chair next to her. "It must weigh thirty pounds. It's too much. Not to mention that thing is hell on your alignment."

"Yeah, but those bags with wheels look so nerdy."

The worst part is, even though I'm a massage practitioner, I agree.

That Friday night, I decide to pull out the stops and fry up a flank steak. The meat sizzles on the cast iron pan as I mash some potatoes with garlic and olive oil. Next comes a grind of cracked pepper across sliced radishes drizzled with olive oil on a bed of arugula. See, if push comes to shove, I actually can cook.

Francisco leaps out of his post on his dog bed and runs over to the stove to stare at me with brown eyes, willing me to give him a bite of steak. He wags his tail: *C'mon, Ma. Gives us a little taste.*

"I am mesmerized by your powers of canine telepathy, Frank, shameless beggar. And who taught you how to do this?" I point to India, who ignores me as I toss him a piece of the fatty meat.

India eats well but doesn't get up from the kitchen table for hours. Her essay is far closer to being done as a result.

Finally, when she gets up looking bleary-eyed, I kiss her sweet cheek and then stagger to my own bed, feeling sore. As I crawl, naked, between the cool sheets, the tension in my body begins to unravel, one limb at time. I sink into the familiar contours of my mattress and drift off to sleep. I realize I am dreaming when I look down to find myself wearing black yoga pants and a red work tank. I am barefoot with my ankle bands on. I stand above a pool of clear water that seems to be cleaved into golden rock. My legs stand hip width apart, my hands rest on my hips. My feet feel cool against the stone as I survey the landscape. I hear a voice from below me some-where say, "Hello."

I look down to find Jean sitting in the pool below me, on a low shelf just off to my left. Her fair tresses are pulled back at the nape of her neck. She wears a long-sleeve form-fitting black jacket made of a coarse, dull fabric almost like a black Brillo pad. The jacket is lined with yellow silk and buttoned securely up to her neck. It covers her only to her upper thigh, leaving her pale shapely legs and feet bare in the clear water. She gazes up at me and asks, "Are you coming to the party?"

I don't answer. Not because I am ignoring her, but because I am admiring the rock surrounding the pool.

She calls up to me again. "Vera, look at me. If you decide to come to the party, I always wear this yellow jacket."

Something wakes me up. I open my eyes. I look up at my dark ceiling. I can still hear Jean's voice saying, "Look at me. If you decide to come to the party, I always wear this yellow jacket."

I know the dream is a message, but I don't yet understand it. Plus, who has the time to remember to research this shit, let alone actually do it? When I look over at my phone, it's 3:32 a.m.

As peculiar as it is, I have to admit that certain aspects of my dreamtime are beginning to play out in my real time. It is not something I can really explain. But sometimes I find myself interacting in my waking life with reconfigured symbols or situations from my dreamtime. I figure this dream business must have something to do with precognition. But why the hell do I want to be clairvoyant when I'm trying to sleep? This is not something that I am ready to accept as a newfound gift, especially in the middle of the night.

However, I am open to the possibility that the dream is a premonition of things that are going to happen at this class. And given the way things have been going with Ernesto and his crew, whatever might shake out up on the ponderosa could be, as India would say, sketch.

VERA

The next Saturday morning, I walk into India's room to find Francisco curled up next to her on her quilt. Both are still asleep. I loop some honey-colored hair behind her ear and say, "I'm leaving, love."

India answers, "Mmm."

"I'll be home by midafternoon tomorrow. There is a lot of food in the fridge. Call me if you need anything. I love you."

"Um-hum, Mama, I sent you a podcast, please listen to it," she says before turning over and going back to sleep.

By the time I leave, I am already a full day late. I chuck my backpack next to my sleeping bag in the back of the car. The backpack holds the only white work tank I've ever owned, even though my intuition keeps nagging me to wear more white when I work. It's so annoying to have this little voice repeatedly pestering me to wear more white, and specifically at this class. Like I even have either the time or the money to go shopping.

I've heard people say that wearing white is like wearing a mirror, as it creates bounceback to denser energies. Some yogis say that wearing white expands your aura to nine feet. I've even met practitioners who will not wear black when they work, but I haven't gotten there yet in my working philosophy. Plus, I am not interested in pausing to listen to my intuition this morning. I am way too busy just getting my butt out the door.

I jump in and blast for the bridge. After I cross the Golden Gate, I claim my spot in the fast lane.

One hour or so later, I arrive, having just digested India's deep dose of podcast viral terror. I roll through Ernesto's gate, pull to a stop, and open my door. As I climb out, his big blonde dog, Luna, sticks her head into my car, looking for Francisco. I leave the door open so that she can sniff around. Out of nowhere, Ernesto materializes and pulls me into a big hug that lasts a beat or two too long.

"Class is about to break for lunch. Would you like to take a stroll with me around the property?"

Not really, but I don't resist. We set off like the friends that we are struggling to be, as I try to give him the short version of the pandemic podcast I just listened to. He half listens, but it seems he'd rather regale me with updates on all of his latest projects. He particularly wants to show me the pool.

It is not until I am standing poolside admiring the artisanship that I flash to the dream that I had last night about Jean. She was sitting on a shelf, wearing a scratchy looking black jacket in a transparent pool of water. There, too, I was busy admiring the stonework.

But I don't really have time to get the implications of this premonition, as Ernesto absorbs my attention yet again. Quietly, he says, "I don't know what's up with Star. I had nothing to do with her being there, Vera. You've got to trust me." Then he sweetens the deal with, "You can stay in the studio as long as you want, baby. But only if you want to." He looks so earnest that I feel tempted to say yes. I am extraordinarily intimidated about leaving, and his offer comes as a huge relief.

Still, I choose to remain noncommittal and head into lunch ahead of him instead. I fill my plate at a buffet that has been laid out in the

kitchen. I sit down at the table and am just in the process of intro-
ducing myself to the other students when out of nowhere, Ernesto
materializes on my right. He links his left foot inside of my right one
and startles me. He cannot be any closer.

This maneuver is so totally out of line, as we've always been dis-
creet about our affections. But most especially when I've been a student in class. Sure, I'll admit to sneaking off to the bushes for a good
grope, but I'm trying to be a grown-up now. And to make matters
worse, Jean is sitting only one person down from me. This is when I
remember a story I heard early on in my apprenticeship.

Once upon a time Ernesto sat next to his current lover at the
dinner table during class. According to this student, Ernesto's hand
had been on his young lover's thigh while Jean looked on sourly.
Again, I can't blame her—it was such bad form. But from my new
perspective, the more remarkable detail of the story is that this young
woman's name was Holly.

This is not exceptional, except that the leaves and berries are actually
the Bach flower plant remedy for the *negative, aggressive feelings directed
at others,* as the basic problem in a holly state is the absence of love.

No shit. As a way of deflecting his advances, I move my plate and
body over as far as I can without sitting in my neighbor's lap. Then
I ask Jean about shamanism. Under the circumstances, it seems like
the only decent thing to do.

She sounds quite happy with her work. Because I am trying to
make nice, I say, "I might like to take a class along those lines," which
is basically bullshit, but before I can finish my thought, Shaman
interrupts me.

"Well, I know where you can find a good instructor."

That same little smile creeps across Jean's face. There is something
about her expression that is really bugging me. I don't know why, but
on an intuitive level, the very last thing I want is to have her anywhere close to my body again.

I shove a bite into my mouth and chew, hoping that the flow of conversation will organically shift. The longer the food sits on my tongue, the more I notice that it is tasteless. After I struggle to finally swallow, I turn to say something to Ernesto, but *poof*, he's gone.

Strange.

Even so, I am still ready and excited to work. I enter the massage room with a familiar sense of anticipation. There is nothing more fun for me than being in a room full of my fellow practitioners, the air gone funky and thick with human connectivity. Anybody who digs this work knows the smell, as it's a fecund and creative scent, signaling the off-gassing of the body's past in order to receive its present.

As I walk through the door to the massage room, however, it hits me. There are only four students in the room, and I know enough about economics to know their combined tuition barely covers the cost of putting on this class. This means that there are only two massage tables set up in a room that normally holds ten.

The space feels solemn. The enormous mirror running along its interior wall refracts an emptiness that exceeds the lack of participants. And there is something else, too: a shabbiness that reminds me of how I've been feeling about our studio.

Ernesto enters to do his demonstration. I've always loved watching him work, but today his demo feels flat and goes nowhere. Bodywork doesn't have to have a destination, but whatever he is up to suddenly seems like fake news.

As he is winding up the session, he asks me to hold the feet of the person on the table. I agree, but as I begin to walk over, Jean catches my eye. All in black with a string of mala beads around her neck, she gets up just off to my left and starts stretching, looking unhappy. But Ernesto and I do this kind of work all the time, so as I take the man's feet in my hands, I figure I'm just making a big deal out of nothing.

Ernesto ends the session and calls it a wrap. He leaves the room, saying he wants to let it warm up. This means that he is obsessively checking his email.

The four students split up into partners and begin working with one another, while I duck into the bathroom for a quick pee. When I return to the massage room, I find Ernesto with a twinkle in his eye and a glass in his hand. In a low voice, he says, "Get on the table, Tex. Just for a minute or two."

Frankly, I adore my nickname. It makes me feel nostalgic as I slip out of my clothes and kick them under the table. I lie face up under the sheet. Shaman pulls a stool up next to me, sits down, and takes my neck in his warm hands.

I love these hands, how hot they feel on my skin—I'm happy to be on the table at this moment—even smelling the bourbon on his breath. I know I've told myself that I am not going to let him work on me while he is altered, but I let it slide one more time because the whole scenario feels so familiar.

I begin to settle into the table, when bang, the door to the massage room opens to reveal Jean. Poised on the threshold, she is caught mid-stride. Seeing me on the table, she bursts into tears.

I peer over the top of my flannel sheet at her, feeling dizzy. I default into my prevailing logic: I am getting gone. Ernesto and I are trying to be just friends. I am leaving the studio—I assume he must have told her that I am leaving. And not to belabor the absolute obvious, but this is, after all, a fucking massage school, lady.

Ernesto looks up at her in vague apology. He mumbles something about how he'll give her some work after he's finished with me. She looks crumpled and hangs around for a moment, watching us. Then she closes the door.

I restrain myself from scratching the recurring itch that is now pestering me like an alarm bell on the side of my nose. I ask, "What was that all about?"

"I have no idea."

Jean seemed really upset, and his habit of dismissing her bothers me as we refocus on one another. I begin to lift my hand to the side of my nose, but Ernesto's paw gets there first. He looks down at me and says, "I'm the only one who is allowed to scratch that itch."

He scratches away. His other hand cradles my neck as I begin to recall my own father's regular drunken visits to my childhood bedroom. Done under the auspices of kissing me goodnight, these visits were my dad's opportunity to unburden his soul of all that was adult and clearly inappropriate for me to hear. Sometimes whatever girlfriend he had at the time would stomp down the hallway to retrieve him, or—and this was even worse—one would whine from his bedroom, "Teddy! Come to bed." In response to her summons, my father, Theodore, would look down at me to say, "She's just jealous."

I had thought these moments with my dad were special. It was pretty much the only time I ever got him all to myself. But now, as I lie on the table rehashing the past, I find that the itch on my nose is becoming intolerable.

Still, I somehow manage to resist scratching it. It is in this space—between the body's wisdom and the impulse that I am not satiating—that the karmic clouds part: Here I am, once again, stuck listening to the drunken father figure, in that the dynamic with Ernesto is replicating circumstances from my childhood. Ah-ha! This moment on this massage table is my cosmic wake-up call.

"Hey, I am thinking of making a movie about my life," says Ernesto. "Do you want to be in it?"

For the first time it dawns on me. Does this guy ever talk about anything other than himself, even while he's working on someone else's body? He chronically talks about his own stuff with his hands on me, but I've been so into him, it's only right now that I am beginning to notice.

I banter back but warily, "Why? Are you going to make a no-budget porn flick?"

I feel anxious as I await his response. But Ernesto is clearly caught up in his own storyline. Remaining unaware of my feelings, he smirks. "Oh, yeah, it's porn all right."

He lets the sentence dangle as he sits there, musing on what this homemade porn might look like. We are now in very uncertain territory.

I have a suspicion that he is referring to Star. I ask, "What are you talking about?"

He doesn't say anything, so I ask him again, "What is it you're even talking about?"

Still, he does not respond. Suddenly pissy, I sit up on the table, look him in the eye, and ask for a third time, "What in the hell are you talking about?"

Nothing. This is super bizarre, especially for a guy who can be so quick. But he is stupefied. Probably, this had a lot more to do with the fact that he is loaded than it does with anything else. He is clearly stuck in sluggish mind, trying to figure out why the bottom has just fallen out between us.

It is this verbal pause that gives me enough space to finally figure out why my neck had been so fucking sore after all those visits from my father. My dad's confidences hadn't felt good to me, but I'd been too young to know that there could be boundaries in intimate relationships. Therefore, I couldn't claim that I didn't like the nightly visits from my dad. How could I? He was my father, my only parent, and I didn't know that fathers could be any different.

Ernesto may have unraveled my tissue with attentive and persistent bodywork, but he too compromised my neck with a mishmash of mixed verbal messages. Today, just for starters, he is fundamentally not respecting my body when he comes to the table lit and probably stoned. The dynamic between him and Jean is confusing and unresolved. And finally, he is talking about something both indirect and unclear while he has his hands on my neck.

How dare he be so careless with my body. I am livid. I get off the table and pull on my clothes.

He comes up behind me and asks, "I thought I was going to work on your neck?" Seeing the *like hell you are* expression on my face, he turns and flees for the laundry room, looking for cover.

I follow him and close the door behind us. Then, with my hands on my hips and my feet spread hip width apart, I give it to him. "What in the hell do you think you're doing?"

He extends his hands palm up. "I have no idea what you're talking about, Tex."

"Stop calling me that! I'm talking about my neck! It's my psychic antenna. You keep bringing up shit that makes me feel anxious while you have your hands on me. This is so negligent as a practitioner. Don't you get it? You're screwing with my intuition. What is wrong with you?" Like a bad boy who doesn't really know why he's in trouble, Ernesto just stands there looking at me balefully with this embarrassed grin on his face. Maybe the reality is that even he, the great maestro of massage, doesn't know what he's doing or what he's talking about. But he teaches this stuff, for God's sake. He should know. Perhaps he is too fucked up or too ashamed or both to simply say so. Either way, I stand there waiting for his response. When I get none, I condemn him with, "Go play these games with your wife."

Why did I even bother to show up under these conditions? I go back into the massage room, feeling disgusted with myself, when it dawns on me that, in the last days, I have lain down for three people with whom I do not feel safe: first Star, then Jean, and now the man I've called Shaman. It has literally taken me three times to finally get myself off the bloody table, but maybe three is, as they say, a fucking charm.

VERA

A little later, the man comes back into the massage room. Looking forlorn, Ernesto waits by our empty table until Jean arrives and climbs onto it, obviously relieved—for once—to be the center of his attentions. I keep my focus elsewhere, as I think things over. None of this dynamic is new news. I was raised in an alcoholic household. I know all about the various constellations: I know all about the codependency; obviously, I know all about the enabling and all about the procrastination, the denial. Obviously why? Because I am still fucking standing here.

But I am here to work, too, so I assist a tentative masseur—he's looking lost as he stands tableside with his female client. I can't have been there for more than a few seconds before Ernesto intervenes. He pulls some heroic-looking moves and orders the woman lying down to begin breathing rapidly. Directing the guy across from me to grab a hand towel from off the hook, Ernesto holds the towel taut between his hands, leans over her, and commands, "Fight me!"

They both begin thrashing and hollering so loudly that I wish I had either a pair of earplugs or an everlasting gobstopper to keep both of them busy. Given the way these two are winding each other up, we are going be here all night. This theatrical battle between the sexes, while fundamentally conceptual, is not going to be resolved on this table. I abdicate my position as witness as she kicks the sheet off entirely.

"The position is too vulnerable," I say as I pull the soft flannel sheet back up over her shaved mound. Looking relieved, the shy guy across from me wipes sweat off his forehead.

Interrupted mid-holler, the woman looks up at me. She and Ernesto both seem disappointed. I lean close to Ernesto and whisper in his ear, "You have to be fucking kidding me."

When I turn away from the table, I see Jean looking happier than she did earlier. She has some color in her pale cheeks as she finishes dressing. Then the man declares, "Let's have a fire ritual." And with that, everybody begins to disband from the two tables and tromp out the door to collect "death arrows and prayer arrows."

I was not thrilled about this ritual the first time around, and that was when I was actually still completely enthralled with the work and the atmosphere. I remember standing by the fire and freezing my ass off, while the whole group listened to some guy reflecting on every single one of his past female relationships as we watched his arrow disintegrate meaningfully. I get that my newfound disillusionment is part of my initiation as a healer. I was curious about healers, their habits, their attire, and their customs, and I have learned an awful lot under Ernesto's auspices. But what I am learning, right now in this massage room, is everything I don't want to do or be as a practitioner.

I then commit my third act of rebellion, blowing off the ritual. Needing a place to hide, I submerge in the Japanese soaking tub, internally and externally simmering.

Yes, massage can have a moment of dramatic emotional release. But only as long as it is the result of a natural progression in bodywork. Indeed, most of our bodies have been on the receiving end of grave indignities to some degree or another, and these indignities deserve attention. But simulated drama with a captive audience? No fucking way.

I leave the tub and drag ass back into the dining area for dinner. Everyone is there, save Ernesto. A couple minutes later, he trips over the threshold, clearly drunk.

Instantly, Jean lurches toward him in an odd crouching motion. Wearing a jacket with a big hood, she looks different, ancient. She holds her elbows tight at her rib cage as she extends her hands toward him. Clutching the front of his shirt, she exhales, "*Thankyousomuchforthework.*"

I am mesmerized by her transformation. I've never seen anyone, let alone Jean, look so haggard. The bottoms of my feet root into the hardwood floor as I realize that I am witnessing her morph into another form of herself—a self she keeps well hidden from every-one if she can. Her desperation is palpable as she slowly releases her hands from the front of her husband's jacket. Then she takes off her coat and turns, having put back on her public face.

Like a well-trained performer, Jean dances her way into the kitchen and beckons us to dinner. I line up to put some food on my plate from a drab looking buffet. When I go to sit down at the table, the room is dead silent; no one is speaking.

Ernesto sits at the head of the table with Jean on his right. In order to create maximum distance from them both, I choose the opposite end. Averting my eyes, I take a bite of some awful vegan something. Dry on my tongue, consistency of sand. I hear Ernesto slur some-thing. Pretending to be oblivious to all of it, Jean pulls her head out of her bowl. With a satisfied smile, she asks no one in particular, "Isn't the mung bean miso good?"

No, I think but do not say.

What family means to each of us is an ever-changing and subjec-tive experience. Of this, I am certain. But at the table tonight, one thing becomes crystal clear to me. I was famished, if not in a state of utter starvation, when I projected my need for a fantasy family with sexy parents onto Ernesto and Jean. Eating under these conditions is hopeless. I give up, take my plate, and add it to the pile in the sink.

I retreat to the massage room and wait for the closing ceremonies. By tradition, each person is going to recap his or her day. Listening to what anyone in this room has to say is the last thing I want to do, but I don't have the guts to just get up and haul ass.

Jean begins by expressing gratitude for the massage she's received.

Thankfully, Ernesto's contribution is equally sober. He feels that his work "has been a learning curve." And the woman feels that her experience on the table earlier that afternoon was, "safe." There you go, ladies and gentlemen. Healing is entirely subjective.

Just as soon as we are done, I make a break for it to Ernesto's man-yurt. I lug the sleeping bag and pillow I've brought from home over to a black shiatsu mat. I push a little pillow aside, thinking it is a very strange choice for something to sleep on, thankful I brought my own pillow and bedding instead. I roll out my old plaid flannel bag.

I punctuate this with an exasperated, "Who the fuck are these people anyway?" I try to get comfortable. But there seems to be something gritty and scruffy underneath me. It makes scratchy sounds every time I shift positions. Both exhausted and hungry, I cry out loud, "How can Jean, the most anal housekeeper I know, have come in here and managed to miss that this mat is covered in fucking gravel?"

Mine is a dark night illuminated only by my rage and my sleeplessness. At dawn, I get up, get dressed, and go to the massage room in the dark morning. The room is frigid. I turn on the heat and sit down on the floor. Poised in front of the mirror and feeling grim, I look at my own reflection.

I begin my daily kriya for cleaning my aura. If I ever needed to clean my aura, it is right fucking now. As I finish, I can hear someone rustling around in the laundry room. I typically would have gone in and asked what I could do to help. But this morning, no way. I remain where I am.

Until the door from the laundry room explodes open to reveal Jean wearing a ratty black fleece hoody that looks suspiciously like a Brillo pad. She jumps at the sight of me standing in the middle of the room, and yells, "*Youscaredmetodeath!*"

When did Jean stop using punctuation?

"*Whatareyoudoing* in the massage room anyway?" she asks. "Students aren't allowed in here before eight o'clock."

Students?

Here we go again. I put my hands back on my hips and spread my feet hip width apart. "I am not his student anymore, Jean."

"You little cunt."

"Cunt?" I ask. "Seriously? It doesn't matter what you call me, Jean. I'm not his student. And I am not yours either. I came up here to assist Ernest in this class. But he got drunk, so I've graduated."

"Like hell you have. You are not his work partner," Jean shrills.

"You are absolutely correct. That was my bad, I am not his work partner. Thank you."

Suddenly livid, Jean lunges toward me, palm open, ready to strike. "He's my husband, you bitch!"

Like I am hailing a New York cabbie, I stick two fingers in my mouth and whistle for all its worth. "Jean! Put on your listening ears. I do not *want* him. Can you hear me? I am no longer competing with you for the man's attentions. You can have him. He is *all* yours." Then I do something I never, ever would have done in the past. I slam the door on my way out.

I stomp back to the man-yurt shaking. I am rummaging around in my bag looking for a trail mix bar, when Ernest appears in the doorway to the yurt. He asks, "Don't I get a hug?"

I know we all say lame things that push each other's buttons, but c'mon. What is the matter with these people? Why won't these two leave me alone? He thrusts a cheese Danish in my direction, asking, "Want a bite?"

"No, I don't want a hug or a bite. I don't want you or your wife in my face either. Why am I supposed to be fucking taking care of the two of you, anyway?"

Then, before I can even consider rescinding it, the proclamation leaps off my tongue. "I'm leaving the studio by the end of this month. I do not want either of you to text, email, or call me after I leave this property."

This could be my version of career suicide, but I'd been up all night thinking about it, and it was long overdue anyway. So fucking bombs away.

Startled by the vehemence of my statement, Ernest slings some shade about how I am being so reactive and jogs off in the other direction, going to find a new audience? Jesus.

As I watch his tight familiar ass recede from my view, I am packing my stuff, throwing my sleeping bag into the car. Then I go looking for him for the last time. I find him outside the massage room squatting over a cardboard box. His black eyes look sad as he asks, "You really don't want me to text or call you?"

It isn't easy, but still I answer, "No, I don't want any contact." I squat down in front of him and put my hands behind his back and pull his body toward mine, lifting him up bodyworker style. I tell him, "Despite all this chaos, I'll miss you."

He presses into me. "I'm going to miss you too, Tex." We stand there, leaning into one another, just breathing, until I let him go.

It's now or never. I have to say it, or I won't feel good about myself. "I lost respect for you as a practitioner yesterday. You can't be loaded when you're working. I don't know what's going on with you, but it's out of hand, and I can't stick around anymore and watch you fall apart. You're a mess. Your marriage is a mess. It's just too painful. I also can't represent your work going forward. I'm sorry."

This is the hardest thing I have ever had to say to anybody. Especially someone I have respected. Ernest has been my teacher, my mentor, my lover, and my work partner. I've also thought of him as my friend. But he is out of alignment when it comes to the tuning of the human body. And by participating, I am out of alignment too.

I walk away, resisting the urge to look back for fear of turning into a pillar of salt. When I hear him open the massage room door and go in, I sneak a last glimpse of the black fabric of his T-shirt. Then I walk over to his lemon tree, pull a plastic bag out of my pocket, pick forty lemons, bag them, and split.

GRACE

The first thing I do when I get home that Sunday morning is to pour the forty lemons into a large bowl hand thrown by the renowned potter Theodore West—my father—whose work abounds in national and international collections. I plunk the bowl in the middle of the slice of redwood that is our kitchen table. Then I throw my sleeping bag and my dirty work clothes next to the washing machine in the garage and walk back down the hall toward my girl's room to say hello.

India's wearing the same pajamas she's had on since yesterday morning and is sitting up in bed with her computer on her lap. As usual, Frank is curled up next to her. In their world, as far as I can tell, it appears as if nothing has changed. I, by contrast, feel like I have just lived twelve lifetimes in the past twenty-two hours. I lean against her doorframe. She looks up at me over the top of her computer. "You OK?"

"Yeah. You could call it that." I give her the skinny, ending with "I've left him. I have to move out of the studio by the end of this week."

Her smile blazes so brightly that I need a pair of shades. "Congratulations, Mom. I am so proud of you! I knew you could do it!" Then she adds, "Did you bring home anything to eat?"

The following Monday morning, I drive over to the T Room to work with a client. When the appointment is over, I take a good look around the joint. It looks pretty much the same too. Nothing has changed here, either. Evidently, I am the only one who is feeling different.

I know it's lame, but I am also feeling a little heartbroken and sentimental as hell; I'd go so far as to say *maudlin*. So I search for a picture frame to put a photo of Ernest and me in. I want to hang it on what is still our wall.

I walk around the studio, looking at photos in a variety of frames. I peer up at the shelf above the kitchen counter and spot a dusty frame that holds an old photo of Ernest and Jean. Aha! Somehow, I just know it's the right one.

The pic has been sitting there for as long as I've been here. Over the last six months, he and I have worked, laughed, and done a lot of excellent fucking under this photo's watchful eye. I'm not proud of this, but it is my truth.

It's too high for me to reach, so I climb up onto the counter, get it, and jump back down to the floor. As I look at it, I think about what a nice shot it is. But, as there is no paucity of newer photos of the two of them together, I decide that the world as we know it will survive with one less.

I open the back of the frame and try to pull out the photo. It's stuck. Looking closer, I notice a piece of wadded up yellow paper stuffed into the back of the frame. I pull it out.

As I unfold it, I discover that the paper is actually a card. On the inside is a note written in careful, girlish cursive. I squint at the writing. But, as usual, I can't seem to read anything anymore without my readers from Walgreen's.

As I walk back to the desk to get my readers, I feel a slight sense of vertigo. Tripping over I don't know what, I bang into the desk, try to steady myself, and simultaneously knock my glasses into the trash. I lean over to fish them out of the pile of snotty tissues.

Lightheaded, I collapse onto the massage chair for a moment to regain my equilibrium. Since my glasses just took a nosedive into other people's germy tissues, I also want to wash them off. I make for the kitchen sink, squirt some lavender dish soap onto the lenses, and swish the bubbles around under running water.

When I dry them off and put them on my nose, the card turns out to be from Ernest's ex-lover, Holly, Bach flower remedy for the absence of love. I linger over its sweetness. Did she take this photo of Ernest and Jean?

In the photo, the two of them are standing side by side up on their property. Ernest is a little in front, Jean leaning her body against him. Her eyes are closed, and she has that same little smile, the one that really bothers me now, playing at her lips.

I look from the card back to the photo, then back to the card, then back to the photo. I see something in the photograph that I have never seen before. The camera has captured, in that split second, exactly what I imagine both of them are thinking.

For his part, Ernest has that "I'll fuck you later." Clearly, it is a facial expression of his that I am not alone in enjoying. What an incorrigible bastard!

Again, I appreciate the depth of this man's sexual appetite, regardless of my common sense. I catch my breath and lean into the kitchen counter. In an extreme act of self-discipline, I drag myself away from his face and onto Jean's. My eyes snag on her expression. It is in this instant that I finally understand. Her eyes may be closed for the purposes of this picture, but in real time, they are wide-open to every single notch on their mutual bedpost.

Jean knows all about his affairs, as it's written all over her face. She leans against him, taunting, *Go ahead, have some, but don't fool yourself. He is mine.* But more pertinent to my situation, she has known the whole time that he and I were lovers. And further, she has used his infidelities with me or with any of his women to fan the blaze of her martyrdom.

Ew protests my stomach. These people are disgusting. I put my left hand over my belly, as I begin to digest all the times Jean dropped hints regarding his boundless infidelities.

Once, during my first weekend of class, she turned to me and casually mentioned that Ernest and some woman had been having an affair, a confidence that then struck me as totally random. It was a pretty public moment to bond over his naughtiness. But I had commiserated—not only did I feel sorry for Jean, but this intimacy made me feel somehow special.

She had also mentioned that she had a habit of internalizing his behavior. As she spoke, she pointed to her solar plexus. Whether it was unconscious or maybe even conscious, she showed me where she was warehousing her feelings on the very subject.

As I look at the photo some more, I realize that this karmic gig is way worse than I'd thought. Jean's martyred identity is, in fact, only the first layer of her veneer, serving as a cloak for her desire to manipulate those around her. The camera has captured an expression on Jean's face that holds something far more sinister than martyrdom. Jean energetically feeds off her husband's relationships with other women. She not only enables him, she's his karmic partner in abuse.

How she does this—or if she is even conscious she does this—is something about which I lack the slightest idea. But I just know it's true vampire.

Has the prescription in my glasses been magically upgraded? How could I have been so blindly naïve? I drop the photo next to the card, attach myself to the kitchen counter, and try like hell to get my bearings. Like a sudden bout of psychic food poisoning, I get hit out of nowhere with a massive wave of nausea. I bend over and dry heave.

For a moment, I just hang out here, my brown hair pooling onto the hardwood floor. I gasp for breath and gently massage my belly. When I stand back up, I begin to get the big-assed nature of this situation. And the worst part is, I totally suited up for it every step of the way. It was in my first class, in fact, when Jean asked me, "Do you know Holly?" Even though Ernest, just like my daddy, had already given me a full download and then some, I said, "No." This was the truth, as I had not met her.

Later, Jean showed me some fabric for making a turban, a gift to her from Holly. She went on to ask, "Do you know a way to get these wrinkles out?"

I am so not handy with these kinds of thing that I wanted to guffaw. That anyone would ever ask the likes of Vera this kind of question? *I had no mother!* In a flash of purest guesswork, I suggested the use of an iron and a damp towel. She ended the moment with, "I knew you would know exactly what to do."

Like I have no clue what she is talking about, but she spent the rest of that weekend wearing that freaking turban, the millinery of his infidelity, around like a helmet.

I assume she doesn't know that he and I are lovers. Because his previous loves that I am aware of have been twenty-something, I just don't fit the profile in that I'm too old. "I am too old for you," I say. He laughs as if this might be true.

From my perspective, Jean doesn't have any reason to feel threatened by me. I don't want to steal her man. I have no intention of marrying him. I only want to borrow him now and again.

Sure, I feel my own confluence of guilt mixed with victory when he takes that photo off the wall that day in the massage room. The victory part is the by-product of competition. But I never like to think of my feelings as a permanent condition. I am a woman. These thoughts are just my momentary flirtation with being a total asshole.

Also, I like to think of myself as being capable of expanding my heart to include the very real probability that my relationship with Ernest might also extend to a form of sexual healing between the two of them. I know it sounds wacky, as we women are so darn hard-wired to compete, but seriously, why shouldn't they have good sex as a result of me? As far as I can tell, things are on the upswing after I show up, in that Jean begins to sport a healthier, more well-laid glow.

My wanton and healthy desire for transformative lovemaking is, in fact, the good news. It is my need to somehow resolve what I project is the breakdown in Ernest's and Jean's marriage—otherwise why would he be fucking around—that presents a problem. What a stupid idea.

As an example, I say to Ernest, "Burn the damn turban."

It isn't that the symbol of the turban is a bad thing in itself, but I imagine Jean is wearing it for all the wrong reasons.

Shaman follows through, suggesting to Jean, "Let's put all of it behind us and burn the turban."

By *all of it,* he of course means his history of falling in love with everyone and, specifically, beautiful young women.

Jean's only response is, "But I love that turban."

No shit she loves the turban; it's a trophy. It represents the luxury of being his wife. Today, as far as I can tell, she actually believes that all his lovers want to marry him. What a load of crap. If there is one subject on which we all agree—and this comes from the horse's mouth—we all think Ernest is way too much fucking work. There is no way in hell that any of us would ever want to be corralled into holy matrimony with this beast.

We just like the bare-assed and free part. This is a maverick concept for Jean. Being his wife is so not the bonus prize. If anything, it is tough duty. I mean why put up with that shit unless she is thriving on female competition? She must be convinced that she has won something.

Now I finally get why that turban resurfaced during class last Saturday with some bling pinned over her third eye like a Christmas tree ornament. Groaning as I remember this, I build a big fire. Then I burn the photo of Ernest and Jean, along with its card. Then I sage the entire enchilada with a smudge stick.

As my eyes squint through the smoke, I decide that I can use my bedroom in our house in the city as temporary studio space. It is a radical decision, but I don't mind sleeping in the kitchen anyway. As if on cue, my cell phone dings three times. I pick my cell up and look at it. Like an act of God every single session I have booked for the day cancels for one reason or another.

I throw in the towel, pick Frank back up, and go home. Later that evening over Tony's pizza, I tell India, "I'm going to use my bedroom as a studio space for a while."

"Mom, are you for real? Where are you going to sleep?"

"In the kitchen. Just until I can find something else, honey."

"I am really happy that you are leaving that dick, but seriously, Mom, my friends are going to think this is so weird."

"What happened to your gift for the capacious overview?"

In a moment of uncharacteristic crankiness, India does not respond. She gets up from the table and slings her plate into the sink. The quick patter of Francisco's toenails in the hallway signals their mutual defection just before she slams her door.

That night, I sweat my way through my sleep, mostly out of fear. I wake up Tuesday morning still feeling fearful. The stiff cup of coffee doesn't help matters on the anxiety front.

Work is sporadic, but I hang on through the rest of the week until Saturday. Before I can abort my world, I have one last client to see. I finish this final session, feeling tragic. So I do what women do, call one another. Me? I call Grace.

She says, "I had a feeling something like this was going to happen."

"What do you mean?"

"Remember when you came over for a drink? I told you that Ernest is simply all about Ernest. That's all there is to him."

Now when I think back to that conversation over that glass of smoky mezcal, her words feel like a premonition.

"What are you, psychic or something?"

"Just get out of there, Vera. I know it's painful in the short run, but take it from me, every single time I've left a man, I've been so much better off."

"But the sex was so good," I tell her, and then I add, "Oh, god, I can't believe I just said that!"

"That's just your lust talking. Of course, it was good. Sensational is even better. I've stuck around every bad relationship I've ever had for great sex. Welcome to being a woman. This is nothing to be ashamed of. Good sex has always been a compelling reason to even bother to be in relationship in the first place."

"I feel like such a child, such a babyish jerk."

"Just get out. I have a bad feeling about your little love triangle. Do you want me to drive over there?"

"That isn't necessary. I can do this."

"Remember, I'm here if you need me."

She disconnects. I've never had a woman have my back before. This feels so new to me as if, in and of itself, it is an act of grace.

I return to my original task and start doing laps from the studio to my car, erasing all evidence of my practice and of my presence in the T Room in Tam Junction.

When I am finished, I tape the photo of the two of us—me and my shaman—to the wall at eye level above our desk, feeling devastated. It is a fitting picture to leave in memory. The woman who took the shot always said it was a lucky accident. The photo says it's no accident.

In it, we are both in focus, standing side by side, while the rest of the image is a blur. We look like the two of us have popped out of a wormhole. The picture catches exactly what and who we are: karmic time travelers whose time has run out.

I walk into the laundry room and open the closet doors. I look at the flannel sheets for the table, stacked high up on the top shelf. Shaman's clothes hang alone below. Stepping closer, I bury my nose in his shirts and take a long, deep inhale before closing the door on his smell.

I walk back into the main room, stretch my arms wide, and take a look around. Remembering everything, I spin a full 360 degrees to my left. When I stop, I am dead center in front of the statue of White Tara remembering the day I brought her here from Polk Gulch Books.

The Tibetan goddess gazes at me. "Want to come?" I ask.

"Yes," she whispers. So, I go to her perch, pick her up, and turn off the lights on my way out.

27
GRACE

The following Sunday morning, I haul my massage table out of the back of the car and up the stairs through the front door into what is about to be my new studio. I called Shorty, the handyman, yesterday. He is going to come over to help me move my dad's bed into the garage later today. This thing is so ancient that the box spring alone must weigh a million pounds.

I've already been to the paint store on Polk and put up a couple of swatches of white. My favorite? Himalayan White. I plan to spend the rest of my Sunday afternoon giving the walls a fresh coat. I want my new home studio space to feel like a fresh start.

I empty out drawers in the dresser to make space for my working tools. Meticulously, I begin to organize the next phase of my practice while I wait for Shorty to arrive.

True to his name, Shorty is slight of stature but strong as a bull. He shows up in a new pair of tan Carhartt's still stiff and unwashed. He singlehandedly wrangles the old mattress into the garage.

"Hey, can you help me bring this table back into my new studio," I ask. Sitting on the table is the golden papier-mâché Egyptian sarcophagus that India built on top of a small human-sized wire armature in fifth grade. She wrapped it in strips of old newspaper covered in a

184

gummy flour-and-water paste. An ambitious project, it took weeks. Once dry, she painted the exterior just like Nefertiti's sarcophagus in hues of cobalt, turquoise, red, and gold.

"Who made this?" he asks.

"India," I say, adding, "naturally."

"Wasn't Nefertiti famous for the length of her beautiful neck?"

"Yep."

"Impressive." Shorty lays India's handiwork on top of the washing machine gently.

Then we pick up the simple table with a single drawer and carry it back into my room and set it down.

"Where?" asks Shorty as he runs a hand over his silver buzz cut.

"How about under the window?"

We place my new desk under the west-facing window. Not much of a view, but the room gets beautiful afternoon light.

When I pick up my wallet off the top of the dresser, Shorty waves me off, saying, "Are you serious? We're family."

I spend the rest of the afternoon painting and puttering. Regressed and childlike, I feel like sucking my thumb. I set up my massage table and put it in the center of the room like an altar. I stretch a shearling pad over it and cover it in cream flannel. Lastly, I put the statue of White Tara on my new desk.

On Monday morning, I take India to school and drive home feeling off. When I walk back into the kitchen, I lay my palm on the unmade daybed, the sheets feeling clammy from the night before. Just to give myself something to do, I decide to strip and wash all the bedding. I haul the armful of sheets from the garage and notice that my unwashed sleeping bag is still sitting there. As I ready it for the washing machine, I start to cry. Tears speckle the bag with dark blue dots.

My grief is not the stuff of a big, rollicking sob fest. More accurately, it is the prevailing onset of an ever-deepening disappointment—I'm despondent that what I believed in is not true. I come back into the kitchen, make the daybed and mope around, doing the dishes from the night before as I wait for the cycle to finish.

The annoyingly cheery tune from the dryer signals its completion. I bring my sleeping bag into the kitchen to re-roll it on my freshly made bed. I toss it onto the white surface, jump back and scream. Black, volcanic grit tumbles out of the sleeping bag; the grit is now strewn all over the virgin field.

For a long time, I stand back and stare at this black debris. It looks exactly like the Brillo pad fabric of Jean's black fleece jacket that she wore at the last class. *What the fucking hell?*

Shaking, I push a pile together with the edge of a dirty dishtowel. Then I grab my cell and call Grace, praying she will answer. The moment I hear her voice, I cry, "I need to talk to you!"

"What's up, Vera?" After I tell her, she inhales slowly. "Jesus. That's for ritual. She's doing ritual."

"Ritual? What the fuck is ritual?"

She doesn't answer my question directly. Instead, she says, "Get it out of your house immediately, Vera."

"What? What are you talking about?"

She orders with more urgency now. "Burn it now, Vera. Take it outside and burn it. Then I want you to strip your bed down to the mattress. Wash everything. Call me back when you're finished."

I hear the line go dead, and I'm frantic. I grab a bag from recycle and scrape the rest of the grit into it with the dishtowel, which is not easy. Almost sticky in its texture, the grit clings to everything it touches.

Once the bag is full, I head for the garbage can outside the garage and throw it away. Frankly, I am too afraid to burn it for fear I might inhale the smoke. I run back inside, snatch the sleeping bag, and throw it back into the laundry basket in the garage. Then I go back and pull apart every component of my bed, down to the mattress itself. For the second time that day, I carry my bedding into the garage.

I move India's precious Nefertiti sarcophagus to a safer place on some deep shelves my dad used for his pots to get it out of the way, before returning to the garage to rotate the selection dial to heavy duty. Walking back into the kitchen to sit down at the cross section of redwood, I lift my right arm and take a good whiff of my armpit; my fear simply reeks. Experiencing the craziest sense of disorientation, I stick my elbows on the table and rest my head in my hands, feeling like my internal GPS is in the process of getting a systems upgrade.

I just used a bag to scrape up this black shit. The bag is shaped a lot like Jean's bag. Jean always says that her bag holds her tools for shamanic healing, but now I wonder if she is actually using these tools for something powerful, bad, something I can't even begin to comprehend.

I think back to her present to me. When I received it, I felt like that kit was somehow my graduation present, but though every time I'm careful to follow the directions, I feel less capable and less confident. Not only that, I actually ended up with something that looked and felt like poison oak on my left hand. Could she actually be using the auspices of a gift to bastardize my intuition? Not to mention poison me?

I recall Jean seeing me on the road just after I finished collecting those turkey feathers. Now I understand that when I offered her those feathers, her expression had been one of triumph. This is the signal of her smile.

This also explains why my hat has no scorpion pin on it. She tore it off while I was in the bathroom!

I shudder to think back to all the times Jean has sent me websites, information, and even once, a map. The map is for directions to a nutritionist. As Ernest says this nutritionist is good, I casually mention being interested in seeing her. That's all it took. I remember getting the map and thinking, *Doesn't she have better things to do with her time?*

For obvious reasons, this is something that bothers me. But it is more than that. In retrospect, it feels like she is trying to wheedle her way deep into my life. To—I don't know—ingratiate herself with me. Unlike Ernest, however, I do not consider her servitude my sovereign due. This servitude actually makes me uncomfortable. I feel like a total jerk. I mean, the wife of the man I am fucking is doing shit for me? And it is shit I haven't even asked for.

Now, it all makes sense. That map, like everything else she touches, is hexed. Every little missive, every little how-to has been a fucking time bomb. This is how she gets her ya-yas: fiddling around with another woman's sense of herself. It just goes on and on.

She could call Ernest a dirty rotten lowdown son of a bitch. Or she could tell him to take a serious hike. Or they could come to some sort of an agreement that he take care of his own business quietly, as infidelity is not something Ernest is ever going to grow out of.

Instead, they propped up the mythos of their marriage, and while he goes about the business of fucking the student body, she gets involved in playing a serious game of hardball with his ladies.

Like me, I hate to admit, she has personalized her husband's behavior. This is our mutual narcissism. Rather than concede that this man is wrapped up in himself, she has made it all about her and the ways she hasn't been able to satisfy him.

Until right now, I did not even know this kind of love triangle could exist. The good news is that I have always been too busy, too disorganized, and too overextended to open those viral links. Nor did I ever visit that nutritionist—I just didn't have the money, the interest, or the time. This means that most of what Jean's sent me is still floating around in the ether of my phone, awaiting activation like some heat-seeking missile sent from enemy terrain.

I look over at the daybed that sits opposite me. I have been fucking him and sharing him with others—particularly this woman—more than six months. I feel gross, physically queasy.

When I think about it, I realize that my health began to rapidly deteriorate about the same time Ernest publicly claimed me as his professional work partner. His declaration took place at a class at their house, and it caught all of us by surprise. By making this announcement, he individuated from Jean. A lot of people were there to witness that transition, including Jean.

It is only now, however, that I am beginning to understand the extent of Jean's wrath. I mean, Ernest was flagrantly careless. He didn't give a shit and demoted her in public after all her hard work. And she, for her part, has been systematically fucking with my body ever since.

The two of them might as well have given me some weird variant in view of the way my immune system has been feeling. He was offloading his arrogance into me while she was actively channeling her need for hateful revenge. And arrogance and revenge are vibrations just like anything else.

I double over, wracked by dry heaves. When my nausea subsides, I slide onto the coolness of my kitchen floor and lie with my ear to the ground. I hear the washing machine signal the end of its cycle. I peel myself off the floor and walk to the garage to put my sheets in the dryer.

After I do, I call Grace back. When she answers, I say, "What the fuck?"

"Tell me everything, Vera."

I tell her about Jean's jacket. I explain that the black grit is the exact same substance that her jacket was made of in my dream. I tell her about finding the yellow card from Ernest's ex-flame Holly—the metaphoric Bach flower remedy for envy and spite. Then I explain what I learned from the photo, concluding that I burned it. She listens, allowing me to unwind the scope of my tale. When I am done, she is silent for a moment before saying, "Jean has been using ritual on you for quite a while now, Vera."

Still not fully understanding what this means, I ask, "What ritual?"

"Ritual is creating bad juju. It is an intimate component of the dark arts. She is practicing black magic to protect her turf. In fact, I don't think she even thinks she is doing anything wrong, which is the saddest part of all."

"But why didn't you tell me?" I ask.

"I didn't know, Vera. I couldn't see it."

"See it?"

"Didn't Ernest tell you? Just like that ass not to do so. I'm an intuitive. By the way, the very same tools that we use to heal can also be used to kill."

I sputter. "They run a fucking school for the fucking healing fucking arts!"

"She misread you, Vera. She doesn't get you at all. In fact, not only does she want to harm you, she hates you. She considers you her equal, her rival. You are a threat to her status quo. Her every intention is to destroy you."

I sit up in my chair. "If his wife is the fucking mother, then we are all up shit creek!"

"True. But guess what? You were the one who chose to be there. Why? And just who *is* the mother if Jean isn't?"

I am too distracted to really hear this last bit. "Does Ernest know?"

"Oh, of course Ernest knows, darling. He just doesn't want to admit to himself that he knows."

I am not sure what is worse: the insidiousness of their behavior or his blind-eye acceptance of it. I have to cop to the latter. He sanctioned their mutual abuse of my body. My feelings of abandonment are complete.

"I am such a total sucker," I sob.

Grace waits for my crying to subside before she says, "Take

everything out of your house that you have received from him personally or professionally. Put all of it into a box in your garage. It is essential that you store everything—photos, books, you name it—until you finally feel absolutely neutral about him."

"Neutral?"

"You will know when you feel neutral. Take all your working tools and clean them with salt. Throw away anything that Jean has ever given you."

"Everything? Even remedies and things that I purchased from her for my practice?"

"Everything is hexed. Hexes are designed to befuddle and confuse. The things that you bought yourself may be OK, but who really knows? Why risk it? She—and he by association—is one hundred percent committed to the destruction of your intuitive capacities."

VERA

Shaken, I trudge to my room to dismantle my new studio space. I take blankets from my closet and spread them out on the deck off the kitchen. Then I take all my working tools—including books, herbal remedies, lotion bottles, surgical tape, tubes of Traumeel, eye pillows, essential oils, bolsters, straps, props—and put everything outside in the sun. After a few minutes, I move the herbal remedies and the essential oils into the shade. Once I sage everything, I dump a carton of Epsom salts on top of the whole shebang.

Now I collect everything that Ernest has given me: anatomical drawings, books, that beat-up flannel shirt, and a card with a love poem by Rumi, the one that says something like, "There is a field beyond right and wrong. I'll meet you there."

Yeah, right, I think. I then pick up what I used to think was sexy. That body jewelry with the two brass amulets in the shape of small flames strung onto a leather thong. Now holding the combination of leather and metal in my hands, I remember how hot I felt when he first put it around my naked hips. I remember how those amulets had found their place. One tucked into my ass cleavage, while the other nestled in what was left of my shorn pubic hair. No thank you.

I carry the chastity belt along with everything else out to the garage. I dump it all into a plastic box along with my handful of greasy turkey feathers. I march back down the hallway and grab my spear. Athena-like, I sweep into the garage one last time and hold the spear aloft in my right hand. Then I plunge it into the box with everything else. I douse every last fucking inch of the contents with another whole carton of Epsom salts. I take a Sharpie, draw a big skull and crossbones on the plastic, and snap the lid shut.

I walk back down the hallway to my former bedroom and look at White Tara. She is sitting on the table Shorty and I brought in from the garage to use as my desk. Aside from Grace—who stands beside me as a spiritual advocate—she is the only witness to my purification process. Tara watches me from her new position on my desk.

I walk out into the kitchen and go through to the deck to pick up that damn essential oil kit by one of its corners. I toss it into a paper bag along with shit that I bought because I was feeling insecure as a practitioner. Like those expensive ankle bands. These bands were like my psychic seat belt. I thought they were helping to keep me focused and grounded in my work, but—in truth—my greatest problem wasn't fancy or costly tools, it was not listening to my own intuition, otherwise known as my common sense. Like every other woman in this fable—save India or maybe Grace—my fear kept me performing, and because I was fearful, I kept buying crap I didn't need.

Once again back in my former bedroom, I take another long look at White Tara. She appears to be presiding over my current circum-stances with an expression of moderate amusement. I gaze into her eyes, ever so thankful that I did not leave her in the studio. The decisive act of throwing my spear may have energized me, but the truth is, underneath this bravado, I feel vulnerable and exposed. I strip down my massage table, grateful that I've got a bunch of smudge sticks. I light a bundle of sage and stick it in a bowl underneath the table. I take the sheets, blankets, and the sheepskin pad into the garage. With the last of the earth-friendly laundry detergent, I begin the next load.

I'm out of laundry detergent. I walk back into the kitchen to get my keys. "Hey, wanna come?" I say to Francisco. He wags his tail, crawls out of his bed, and does his rendition of down dog. Discounting the morning ritual of my cleaning my aura, Frank's the only one around here with a regular yoga practice.

Leashed up, the two of us walk down to the hardware store on Polk Street. The first thing I see when I walk in the door are boxes of AH Epsom salts. Neatly stacked at eye level, these boxes are packaged in what look like milk cartons. I burst out laughing. It is more from the stressful absurdity of my situation than from everything else. There is a euphemism in AA that says, "You don't go to the hardware store looking for a carton of milk." These cartons are my reminder that I have been looking for love in all the wrong places. Ernest convinced me that he was more grounded, more real, more loving, and a whole lot less crazy than the family I already had. Now I get to ask myself, *How much Kool-Aid can one grown woman drink?*

Gallons, evidently. I load up on four half-gallon cartons, seriously questioning if this is going to be enough. Then I grab laundry detergent, some spools of copper wire, and some copper nails.

When we get to the checkout counter, Francisco gets up on his hind legs and does his little circus slut dance for a treat. Anybody who has a mutt knows that every day is like Halloween for a dog in the city of San Francisco. The woman behind the counter hands him a tiny, pale-green dog-bone-shaped cookie full of all the wrong ingredients. Frank chomps on the junk food with satisfaction. I swipe my debit card and begin the walk back to my house.

I make it to the corner as if I have just done the first leg up Everest. A café up the street beckons. Succumbing to the weight of my spiritual load, I claim this café as my basecamp and collapse onto the bench outside.

I've heard somewhere that there are correspondences between planets and metals in astrology. I don't know why I am thinking about this but, as usual, I am curious. I pull out my cell and Google. The list runs from inferior to superior. Saturn equates with lead, Jupiter with tin, Mars with iron, Venus with copper, Mercury with mercury, the moon with silver, and the sun with gold. According to my phone, the correlation between the two, planets and metals, symbolizes cosmic energy in solidified form. I remember flailing around in some kundalini class when the scraggle-bearded yogi with the turban said, "At its most essential, the libido is cosmic energy." Great—so-called cosmic sex energy has gotten me into an awful lot of trouble.

Who knew that my sex drive would park me on a bench on Polk Street with a bag full of salt, ruminating on planetary correspondences so I don't have to go home and do more spiritual laundry? I think about my scorpion pin. I liked that pin a lot, loved it in fact—and I want it back. Just thinking about where it is now gives me a stomachache. But according to Wiki, this pin is tailormade to protect me. Crafted out of silver, it's correspondent to the moon.

I lean over to look at my dog and say, "Frank, the moon is actually my ruling planet! I'm a Cancer. The silver has been acting as my shield."

He looks up at me, wags, and lifts his haunch to pee on the bench leg for the third time. Plus, the scorpion has turquoise on its hind parts. According to my science phone, turquoise is a copper-based, high-frequency stone. Copper is aligned with Venus, the ruling planet of love.

Now I need to know what scorpion means. It is a totem focused on claiming vulnerability, creating protection, and releasing old baggage. Scorpion medicine equals transformation with a capital T— nobody ever said transformation is easy.

The T Room. Ha! I stand up from the bench in front of the café feeling empowered by this new slant on things. I lift my hefty bag for the second phase of my climb. By the time I reach the cleaners on the next corner, I need to switch my bag from one hand to the other.

David Yee owns the cleaners, and I've known David my whole life. Spotting me struggling, he comes outside to ask, "Need help?"

"No, David, I got this."

He glances in the bag. "Whatever you're doing, it looks expensive."

"I know. I'm cleaning."

"What's the copper for?"

"It's good for grounding."

David smiles at me like he thinks I'm a little insane. Of course, I am. But I'm the one who has gotten myself into this pickle, and I am just going to have to be my own Sherpa.

When I reach our house, I drag my bag into the kitchen. As I turn to put my house keys back into the key bowl, I notice that, what with all the drama, I have forgotten to take the studio key off my key ring. As I jimmy the key off, I find myself holding it in my right palm.

According to my science phone, there are certain rites where a person "is required to divest himself of his metals . . . because they are symbolic of his habits, prejudices, and characteristics. These can be things like coins, keys, or trinkets."

I look down at Francisco and say, "No fucking shit."

Playfully, he rises up onto his haunches to do his circus act again. We dance a little around the kitchen before I decide to nail that fucking key to the wall of my kitchen. I slam that puppy into the first stud I can find just to remind myself of what I don't want to do in my next relationship. Then I bust a spool of copper wire out of its plastic wrapper because I'm taking no prisoners. I wrap a bunch of it around my wrists and ankles for increased protection. Next, I pop open a carton of Epsom salts. I'd always heard it was good for cleansing but what the hell, I Google away. The salt crystal is defined as both "spiritual and neutral."

Perfect, right? Didn't Grace say I had to be absolutely neutral? I am going to be so fucking neutral that I'm not even going to be able to recognize my non-neutral self.

I carry the carton out my front door. In what I have now conceived as my practical quest for neutrality, I proceed to salt the entire exterior perimeter of my house. I focus particularly on the thresholds, ultimately using three and a half out of the four boxes.

I've made a reasonably wide barricade with the glittering crystals, and I am just putting on some finishing touches when India walks up. She stops in front of me and asks, "Holy fuck, Mom, what are you doing?"

"Long story, sweetie."

"Like, tell me something I don't know. Your whole life is one big, long fucking story."

"What's up with you?"

"What's up with me? My mother is dumping salt all around our house like some insane person, and what's up with *me*?"

India steps over the heavily salted perimeter and enters our house. She tosses me a backwards glance that naturally conveys that her mother's cra-cra. And I am. And this is only the beginning.

Once I'm done salting, I go inside to find India in the kitchen with her head in the fridge. She selects a yogurt, pulling back the foil. As she leans against the wedging table, her spoon poised in her hand, she listens to me recount my tale. Carefully carving the spoon across the creamy surface, she savors her first bite and says, "Mom, this sounds just like school."

"What do you mean?"

"I mean Ernest and Jean's behavior is not all that far off from what I've been putting up with from my beloved 'peers' forever."

"Seriously? It's that bad even in high school?"

"Where have you been?" Her point made, she yanks a bag of potato chips out of a bowl on the wedging table and departs for her bedroom to go do her homework with Francisco.

As usual, dumbfounded by her exceptional capacity for coherence, I go out onto the deck to retrieve my tools from their hiatus in the sun. I leave the salt-covered blankets outside. Exhausted, I call Tony's for a margarita and salad delivery at five o'clock. Afterward, I take an exceptionally long and overdue shower. By eight, I've keeled over onto my bed in the kitchen, my hair wet, my extremities wrapped in copper.

WHITE  TARA

I awaken to Tuesday. I Google what Tuesday means just for the hell of it before I even bother trying to get out of bed. Tuesday is a day related to Mars, the planet of war. "See?" I say, looking at the screen defiantly. This qualifies as one of those days when it might be simply safer to remain horizontal.

I spent most of last night thrashing around in some kind of bardo. Google defines the bardo as the Tibetan's concept of purgatory. Does eight hours of struggle between waking and sleeping, obsessing over the loss of my old reality and the prospect of my current financial insecurity count? And my sheets are soggy again. If it can be possible, I feel worse. Naked, I finally get up to find myself conveniently located near the refrigerator, the new bed having some perks. I wrap a couple of cold slices of pizza in foil for India, and then I dress. I drive India and Francisco to school.

After dropping her off, Frank and I drive home. He follows me into the garage as I transfer the sleeping bag into the dryer and throw my sopping sheets into the wash. I walk back into my new studio and sit down at the desk in front of White Tara. I decide to send out an email to the few clients I have scheduled this week telling them that I am currently in the middle of a domestic crisis of unprecedented proportions and that I need to reschedule. I close my laptop feeling uneasy. I walk into the bathroom to fill the tub sprinkled with the last of the Epsom salts.

As I listen to the sound of the running water, I feel an urge to call Grace. I am craving a good long bitch session and want to assault her with exactly what I think of that goddamn bitch and her awful user of a husband. By now, I have at least one hundred opinions about Jean's behavior. I mean, this is a subject that I can really sink my teeth into. My whole house is upside down. I have done more laundry in the last twenty-four hours than I've done in weeks. I have salted the entire perimeter of our house to ward off evil. Plus, I am about to drench my body, which I now have considerable questions about, in the remainder of the fourth box of Epsom salts.

Naked, I sit my ass down on the toilet seat as I wait for the water to rise. I am actually getting a lot of energetic satisfaction out of juicing my resentment. Hell, it's a lot easier to blame my current conditions on that hag than it is to own up to that man's participation or, even worse, my own.

But the longer I sit here feeling victimized (on what my father charmingly referred to as "the throne"), the more I also begin to notice that, physically, I really am feeling terrible.

OK, granted, I didn't feel swell when I got out of my sweaty bed. But the feeling had seemed more a result of my emotional state. Now, I feel all kinds of physical symptoms. My throat hurts, my muscles ache, and my entire left side—which they say is home to my intuition—feels sore and congested.

"This is all I fucking need," I holler to anyone who might be listening. I get off the pot, turn off the faucet, and walk my nakedness, extremities still encircled in copper, into the kitchen. I squeeze one of my forty lemons into a glass of water. Gulping most of it, I return to the bathroom with the alkaline-inducing remainders of my glass and climb into the tub.

As I float around the baptismal, alchemical waters composed of approximately the same ingredients as my own tears, I make the not insignificant observation that whenever I have what some teachers would call "mean-spirited" thoughts, I feel worse. In other words, I am being made physically ill by my malicious shit-talk.

My internal impulse to royally blame and grouse and bitch is only further embedding these very same feelings in my body. This, after everything else, is just so not fair! How do I put a serious choke chain on the neck of my impulses?

The unfolding scope of what some people like to call their karmic assignment takes on new, if not colossal, proportions. Can't somebody else do their bit to change the nature of the human condition? I mean *why fucking me*?

I emerge from the tub feeling the greatest sense of resolve I have experienced since yesterday. I throw on a pair of white jeans with blown out knees and a white T-shirt. I circle my grandmother's turquoise and silver bracelet on my left wrist behind the copper and head for the garage to pull the sleeping bag out of the dryer and transfer my sheets.

When I drag the bag into India's room to roll it up on her bedroom floor, a feeling grazes the back of my neck. I dismiss it, assuming that, by this point, the bag has just got to be clean. But when I throw it down, more black grit spills out of it, onto a patch of sunlight on India's rug. Furious, I snatch the sleeping bag, march into the garage, and fling open the door into our driveway. I hurl the sleeping bag out over the salt barrier, as far away as I can. I shout after it, "Fucking A, fucking B, fucking C!" Something stops me from going through the whole alphabet. I stop at C. C for compassion, remember.

I go back into my studio and look at White Tara. "Why me?"

That smile still seems to play at her rosy, girlish lips. Why does she think this is funny? What did I ever do to deserve this new chapter of what the people in the Bay Area like to call my fucking dharma?

I stare back into White Tara's eyes. This black-haired bodhisattva is offering me an alternative—to the hell realms of humanity's behaviors—inclinations like lust and competition that not only magnetized that sham man and his wife to me, but also created this fucking planetary virus. I mean the thought that some dude in Wuhan, China, may have eaten a pangolin infected by a viral bat because he thought it was an aphrodisiac.

Why aren't people shouting, "How was the hard-on, motherfucker?"

Now the damn virus is upon us—not so different from Ernest and Jean's—and it threatens to decimate a planet propelled by competition and the male libido.

OK, so I've inherited an antiquated skill set from my father. Like who hasn't ended up with something from their parents—including this virus—that they'd rather not have? I'm walking around with a set of coping mechanisms that I don't need anymore, swearing being the least of my worries. It is almost as if this goddess is saying to me, "Consuming fear and doubt is a choice. Choose C for choice."

What a novel concept. Do I want to embrace the happy reflection of a goddess? Or do I want to keep focusing on Ernest and Jean and their version of the coronavirus? The choice really is mine.

I choose the goddess. I decide to Google her and read, "Tara symbolizes the power of aspiration, spiritual ascent, and the potential that is actualized through transformation."

I go get a votive candle and a glass holder from the kitchen. I place them in front of Tara. I light a match and try to ignite the candle in front of her. It illuminates briefly; then it sputters and fizzles out. Assuming it is a dud, I go to the kitchen and get another candle. I place the new one in front of White Tara and strike a second match. But this candle fizzles too. Aggravated, I retrieve another candle. When I try to light this third one, it does the same thing.

I get it. This icon was in that old studio. She is hexed too. She is in the same condition as I am. We both need cleaning. "Hold on," I say. "I'm going to build you an altar."

Once I get started, it's not all that complicated. Like most things, it becomes more about my intention—I just hate that word sometimes—than anything else. I decide to use stuff I already have.

Francisco reconnoiters his spot in the kitchen as I head for the deck. There, I find a red ceramic stool covered in dirt. I hose it down, wipe it off with a rag, and lug it into my new studio. Then, in a drawer in the kitchen, I find an old white table napkin that has some colorful embroidery along its edges. I lay it on top of the stool. Next, I pick some rosemary from the plant by our front door and put the sprigs in a little glass vase on top of the napkin. When I place White Tara in the middle, she looks pleased. In front of her, I set a new votive candle in a glass holder.

I position myself on the floor in front of my new altar, sitting with legs crossed. We called it Indian style in kindergarten. It's probably not considered PC anymore, but it is the closest I am ever going to get to full lotus. The position of my body is a reflection of White Tara's own. I stare at her lovely breasts, her green harem pants, and the golden headgear of a tenth stage bodhisattva that crowns her raven head. At this point in my female evolution, my body is not looking quite as perky as hers—why am I even comparing? One thing is looking up on my end—the knot in the back of my heart is no longer throbbing. Tara is going to be my teacher. She is going to show me how to recover my compassion for myself. My job is to simmer down and listen.

I pick up a box of kitchen matches, select one, and strike. I extend it toward the wick of the candle as I hear the spontaneous sound of my own voice chanting: *Om Tare Tu Tare Tu Re So Ha.* "Om! O Tara! I entreat, O Tara! I entreat you, O Tara! O swift one! Hail!"

As I look deeply into the reflection of Tara's benevolence, a cascade of little white stars shoots out from her headgear, illuminating her altar. She closes her eyes and smiles as the wick ignites and the flame takes hold.

Acknowledgements

To Jane Vandenburgh and Linda Watanabe McFerrin, my writing instructors, thank you for your patience, wisdom, and trust. To Brooke Warner, Lauren Wise, and Krissa Lagos at She Writes Press, thank you for your support, and intelligence. To Crystal Patriarch, Keely Platte, and Hanna Lindsley, the Book Sparks team, thank you for your smarts and sensitivity. To my extraordinary group of female readers, thank you for your keen eyes, and direction. To Matthew Felix, thank you for your know how. To Ruth Gumnit, thank you for your clarity. To the author John Blofeld, thank you for the beautiful book, *Bodhisattva of Compassion*. To my precious daughter, thank you for your exceptional feedback! As to my husband, without your love, your friendship, and your excellent sense of humor it would not be possible to write at all.

About the Author

Victoria Lilienthal has studied and practiced body-based work and been certified in sound healing. Long captivated by myths, symbols, and rituals, her studies and mentorship with cultural anthropologist Angeles Arrien, helped to inspire this book. A San Francisco native, she lives in Northern California along with her husband, and their senior citizen dog. *The T Room* is her first novel.

SELECTED TITLES FROM SHE WRITES PRESS

She Writes Press is an independent publishing company founded to serve women writers everywhere. Visit us at www.shewritespress.com.

The Geometry of Love by Jessica Levine. $16.95, 978-1-938314-62-9
Torn between her need for stability and her desire for independence, an aspiring poet grapples with questions of artistic inspiration, erotic love, and infidelity.

The Black Velvet Coat by Jill G. Hall. $16.95, 978-1-63152-009-9
When the current owner of a black velvet coat—a San Francisco artist in search of inspiration—and the original owner, a 1960s heiress who fled her affluent life fifty years earlier, cross paths, their lives are forever changed . . . for the better.

Shanghai Love by Layne Wong. $16.95, 978-1-938314-18-6
The enthralling story of an unlikely romance between a Chinese herbalist and a Jewish refugee in Shanghai during World War II.

Size Matters by Cathryn Novak. $16.95, 978-1-63152-103-4
If you take one very large, reclusive, and eccentric man who lives to eat, add one young woman fresh out of culinary school who lives to cook, and then stir in a love of musical comedy and fresh-brewed exotic tea, with just a hint of magic, will the result be a soufflé—or a charred, inedible mess?

Tasa's Song by Linda Kass. $16.95, 978-1-63152-064-8
From a peaceful village in eastern Poland to a partitioned post-war Vienna, from a promising childhood to a year living underground, *Tasa's Song* celebrates the bonds of love, the power of memory, the solace of music, and the enduring strength of the human spirit.

The Lucidity Project by Abbey Campbell Cook. $16.95, 978-1-63152-032-7
After suffering from depression all her life, twenty-five-year-old Max Dorigan joins a mysterious research project on a Caribbean island, where she's introduced to the magical and healing world of lucid dreaming.